LYRA, my LOVE

LYRA, my LOVE

by
Jan Tempest

MOODY PRESS

CHICAGO

Printed in the United States of America

1

"YOU'RE BEAUTIFUL, Lyra. The loveliest girl I've ever seen," Mike said huskily, reaching for my hand under the table. "I'm crazy about you—"

I eluded his groping fingers and shook my head impatiently. I must have been crazy to have accepted his invitation for tonight. When he had called me, he had talked vaguely of a party. He must have known that I would never have agreed to go out with him alone. My family would have been horrified at the idea. Mike O'Donnell might be the mayor's only son, but his reputation in Kelchester was far from shining—to put it mildly.

Probably his wild escapades had been exaggerated. I didn't suppose that there was any real viciousness in Mike. He was young and gay and handsome, just graduated from the university, with too generous an allowance from his indulgent father, and taking a break before he settled down to work in his father's construction company. He was popular in Kelchester, but not in the Cathedral set. I had met him occasionally during his vacations, and found him pleasant enough, but this was the first time I had ever been out on a date with him. It would be the last time too, I resolved grimly, if this popular roadhouse was his notion of a suitable setting for Archdeacon Haughton's daughter.

My father liked to call himself broad-minded, but he drew

rigid lines for his wife and daughters. We were allowed to go to concerts and to parties at friends' houses or in aid of charity and to certain serious or Shakespearean plays. Operas performed by the Kelchester Amateur Operatic Society were permissible too. But we could only be spectators; he had sternly forbidden me to join the society.

We had had an argument about that. I didn't normally question Father's edicts. I had given that up in my teens when I had discovered the hard way that I was merely bruising myself against a stone wall. My yearning to sing—anything and anywhere—was too strong to be suppressed though, and I had begged him to let me be in their autumn production. Mother had added her pleas to mine, saying that plenty of our friends supported the society. It was surely a harmless way of spending the long evenings, she had reasoned, but Father had remained adamant.

He had quoted one of his favorite texts: "All things are lawful for me, but all things are not expedient: all things are lawful for me, but all things edify not."

It would not be dignified for the archdeacon's daughter to make a public exhibition of herself on the stage, he assured us, and music had too great a hold over me as it was. I had a nice voice, certainly, he had continued, but I should not allow it to go to my head. It was a gift to be used in God's service, not for my personal vanity and gratification. I could sing in the choir and I belonged to the Music Club; that should be enough for me.

It was useless to protest that it wasn't nearly enough and that he made me feel like a caged lark. We didn't sing at the Music Club; we merely attended concerts. I enjoyed them, but I longed to make music, not just to listen to it. I ought to have been at a club concert tonight with James Mallard. The club's monthly meetings were quite a social occasion in Kelchester, with a get-together and refreshments after the concert. For the past two years, ever since I had gone to work in his father's office as a secretary, James had escorted me to the concerts. He wasn't a demonstrative man, but he had made it clear that he regarded me as his girl. I was sincerely fond of him, and my

6

parents had seemed to approve of the embryo romance between us.

Perhaps I wasn't in love with James, but I liked him a lot better than any other man I knew. I had taken it for granted that some day, when his father took him into partnership, we would be married. It had come as a shattering shock to learn that he had invited my younger sister to tonight's concert. Dorothea had accepted the invitation eagerly and been mildly triumphant about it. I had been completely baffled because Dorothea didn't care for any form of music, and I would have expected her to find a concert of chamber music an endurance test. Until now James had barely noticed Dorothea. What on earth was the idea?

On an uncontrollable impulse, I had asked him about it in the office yesterday morning. He had looked uneasy and embarrassed.

"I thought it might be as well," he had said, staring down at his desk. "To make a break, I mean. You know how people talk."

"The club members will certainly talk when you turn up with my sister instead of with me," I had assured him tartly.

"That's just it! People are beginning to pair us off together, Lyra, and that's not a good thing—for either of us," he had answered awkwardly. "It's not as if we were engaged—or likely to be."

"Aren't we—likely to be?" I had blurted out, my throat suddenly dry.

He had given me a swift harassed glance, and color had risen dully to his face.

"You know my situation. I've only been a qualified attorney for eighteen months. Father won't give me a partnership for another two years, at least. Until then, I can't possibly commit myself," he had said impatiently. "You're a very lovely girl. If people imagine you're tied down to me, it'll spoil your chances, as Father says."

"So, this is your father's idea? He doesn't want you to be tied down to me? Why not?" I had demanded, bewildered as well as hurt.

7

"He has his reasons." James had paused and then added uncomfortably, "Nothing personal, of course. He just thinks it would be wiser for us to see less of each other outside of office hours."

"And wiser for you to see more of my sister?" I had flung at him.

"Why not?" His color had deepened, but his tone had been even. "My father isn't only your father's legal adviser; our families have been friends for many years."

"I had certainly thought that you and Mary were my friends."

"Naturally. But does that mean I have to exclude your sister? Why shouldn't I take Dorothea out occasionally? According to Mary, Dorothea doesn't have all that many dates. It's a bit tough on her to be always outshone by you," he had retorted defensively.

"You're becoming awfully chivalrous over my sister. That's something new." I hadn't been able to keep the bitterness out of my voice. "You couldn't be more wrong, James. Dorothea is the family favorite; Father and Aunt Clara dote on her."

I had checked myself there—or pride had checked me. Nobody except Mother, and perhaps our dear old organist and choirmaster, Arthur Devereux, knew what it was like for me at home; the constant complaining and the chilly disapproval which I had to endure from my father and his unmarried sister. Try as I would, I could never measure up to their exacting standards in the way my sister did. Dorothea was "a real Haughton," as Aunt Clara was fond of saying. Both in looks and temperament, Dorothea was a younger facsimile of Aunt Clara, tall, fair, self-controlled, self-possessed and practical, with no artistic or emotional streak in her.

I was a throwback; a misfit. I wasn't in the least like the Haughtons. I didn't take after Mother either. She was a quiet, retiring and gentle little woman who never appeared to resent being ordered around by her forceful husband and sister-in-law. She had light brown hair, graying now, and brown eyes. My bright auburn hair and green eyes must have come from

8

some remote ancestor, like my voice, and my "dangerously impulsive, emotional nature," as Aunt Clara called it.

"Lyra, you're not listening. You look as if you're miles away," Mike said reproachfully. "What's on your mind?"

"Sorry, I was just thinking," I said hurriedly.

"Not about me." His tone was half amused, half piqued. "The girls I date don't usually look through me as though I'm invisible."

"But, I'm not the kind of girl you usually date," I said ruefully. "And this isn't my kind of place. Honestly, I'm sorry, Mike, but could we go now?"

"Go?" he echoed, raising his brows. "Go where?"

"Home, please."

"In a minute. We haven't even had coffee yet. What's wrong with this place?"

I glanced helplessly around the crowded room. It was difficult to put my uneasiness into words. The food and service were undeniably excellent, and the decor was colorful and pleasing. I knew nothing against the roadhouse; in fact, I hadn't even heard of it before. It was on the main London road, about twenty miles out of Kelchester. From the way the head waiter had greeted us, Mike was obviously well known here, and he had told me that he and his friends came here often. Several couples whom I hadn't recognized had waved to him as we had been shown to our table. Was that why I had this uncomfortable feeling? Maybe it was an intuitive sense that a setting familiar to Mike's friends would seem highly inappropriate to Father and Aunt Clara.

"It's very hot," I said lamely. "There's such a crowd—"

"All right. We'll have coffee in the lounge. Anything to bring a smile to your lovely face." Mike grinned, and signaled to our waiter.

"Thank you," I said gratefully, forcing a smile.

He paid the bill and we headed for the door. I was conscious of curious or speculative glances directed at us as we passed.

I tried to ignore them, but I heard one man murmur to his date, "Mike's got a new girl. Good-looking too. Who is she?"

"You'll never guess. Get ready for a good laugh. She's old Archdeacon Haughton's daughter," his companion retorted.

I felt my cheeks burning. As Mike held the door for me, I wished again that I had refused his invitation instead of letting hurt pride goad me into accepting it. I couldn't shake off a conviction that by coming out with Mike this evening I was guilty of disloyalty to my father, and I had always tried to be loyal to him.

It seemed terrible to have to admit it, even to myself, but I didn't love Father. I couldn't. It wasn't entirely my fault either, for he had never sought my affection and had never shown me any. Even in my childhood he had been severe with me, making no secret of his preference for Dorothea. Years ago I had supposed that it was natural for parents to make a fuss over the baby of the family, but gradually it had dawned on me that my father had no love to spare for his older daughter. I had been a high-spirited, mischievous child, but I had always responded instantly to any emotional appeal.

Mother had only to say, "I'm tired, don't worry me now, darling," and I would be as quiet as a mouse.

I loved my mother devotedly and had never doubted her love for me. She had always tried to shield me from Father's wrath, and make excuses for me when I had annoyed Aunt Clara. Because of her pleading, I had been allowed to take singing and piano lessons at school. If the decision had been hers, I could have made music my profession instead of being a secretary in a dreary attorney's office, but she had been no match for Father and Aunt Clara.

For Mother's sake I had curbed my rebellion against Father's harshness and continued to live at home instead of going out on my own as I had longed to do. I couldn't stand to grieve Mother. But sometimes I wondered if life wouldn't be easier for her if I were out of Kelchester. No matter how hard I struggled to conform, I seemed fated to be a discordant element in the family. Perhaps I should have made the break when I was twenty-one, but there had been James—or so I had imagined. Now, even James had failed me.

10

"I'll just get my coat," I said hurriedly, as Mike reached for my arm.

"What's the hurry?" he frowned.

"Father expects me to be in by midnight."

"And you're—how old is it? Twenty-one?"

"Twenty-three next month."

"Ridiculous! He can't treat you as if you were sixteen," he protested. "Why do you stand for it?"

"Because if I upset him, he takes it out on my mother," I answered, irritated by the hint of scorn in his tone. "That's why."

I dived into the cloakroom and got the dark green coat which matched my plainly cut but lovely brocade dress. I had an inborn flair for color and line—another score against me in Aunt Clara's eyes. She complained that I spent too much on my clothes and tried to look like a fashion model. It didn't matter to her that it was my own hard-earned salary that I spent. She seemed to think it was positively wrong to make the best of oneself, and she never wore anything but browns and fawns and grays—inconspicuous and durable. Dorothea followed her lead in that, as in most other things. They prided themselves on always looking "ladylike." That they also looked dowdy and old-maidish didn't appear to occur to them. Neither could understand my craving for warmth and color, my chafing against the restrictions with which Father hedged us about, or my impulse to live life to the full while I was still young. I realized that we had to consider Father's position, but did that mean that Dorothea and I had to behave as if we were middle-aged?

Dorothea and Aunt Clara were prone to discuss earnestly what was and what wasn't fitting for "professing Christians." I didn't doubt their sincerity, but I had a strong if muddled feeling that Christianity shouldn't consist of upholding petty rules and mercilessly criticizing anyone who broke them. Christianity should surely mean having a heart full of love and compassion. Aunt Clara was indubitably a "good" woman, but Mother was much more my idea of a Christian. Father was, to me, the present-day version of one of those formid-

11

able, unbending Old Testament prophets, firmly driving his flock rather than leading it. One had to admire his integrity and single-mindedness. He had a good mind too, and was a wonderful organizer. I was proud of my father, but there was no joy for me in being his daughter.

With a stifled sigh, I stepped out into the corridor again—to have my arm grabbed by Mike.

"Come on! Let's get out of here!" he said urgently, hustling me unceremoniously down a side passage. "There's a French window in the billiards room. We can slip out that way."

"But—but—why?" I stammered, bewildered by his sudden change of tune.

"Police!" he answered succinctly.

"Police?" I echoed blankly.

"A friend of mine—Harry Grenley—just told me that he saw the police car."

We were almost running as we dashed down the passage and into a big, deserted room with shrouded tables. He left the door open, but only a little light penetrated. We bumped into a table as he dragged me across the room.

"I don't get it," I said breathlessly. "What have the police to do with us?"

"Nothing—but do you want to be interviewed and have them take your name and address? There's bound to be a reporter along," he said rapidly, pushing at the lock of the French window. "How do you think my father—and yours— would react if they saw our names in the paper as being among those present? Use your head!"

My heart began to thud as I followed him out into the cool night air. I couldn't understand why the police would suddenly descend on this busy, thriving roadhouse, but I didn't need to be warned of my father's reaction to my being present, however innocently, when they arrived.

We had come out on a path which appeared to lead through shrubbery. The moon had risen and, as Mike hurried me down the path, I caught a glimpse of dark, scurrying figures ahead of us.

"We can get to the parking lot this way," Mike explained in

a lowered tone. "With any luck, we can get out without them knowing it."

I didn't like this sneaking out the back way as if we were criminals, but I decided that the alternative would obviously be worse. I had been a fool to come out with Mike at all; he seemed to attract trouble like a magnet.

When we reached the parking lot, he pulled me along behind a row of parked cars, urging me to keep my head down. By a devious route, we reached his fast, showy sports car. He pushed me inside, closing the door with exaggerated care and only the slightest click. Then he sprang in beside me and started the engine without switching on the lights. He began to nose the car forward, and then suddenly moaned.

"Oh, no! They've got a man at the exit. Look! He's stopped Harry," he said ruefully. "Hang on!"

By the overhead light at the parking lot entrance, I saw a burly policeman standing beside a car, examining what I guessed to be the driver's license.

Then I caught my breath sharply. Mike had switched on his headlights and was revving up the engine. Instead of drawing in behind his friend's car, he was accelerating and heading for the exit. There wasn't room for us to pass—and the policeman was holding up his hand.

"Stop! Mike, you must stop!" I gasped, sensing his intention.

"Hang on!" he said again, and drove straight at the policeman.

For one horrible moment I was terrified that Mike was going to run down the policeman. But, in the last split second, the man swiftly stepped aside. There was a terrible jolt as one side of Mike's car scraped the gatepost. Then we were out on the road, driving recklessly in front of an approaching car, and racing toward Kelchester.

"Mike, you—you idiot!" I burst out, shaken and indignant. "You could have killed that man."

"No chance! Don't panic," he said curtly. "He saw I meant business."

"Yes, but why? Why couldn't you have stopped and shown

him your license? Why this panic?" I demanded. "What is it all about, anyway? We haven't done anything. The police wouldn't have bothered with us—"

"That's all you know!" I'm not exactly a favorite with them."

"Oh, I know you've been fined for careless driving, but the police surely didn't come there to check up on drivers," I said confusedly. "What was it? Something to do with their liquor license?"

I really didn't know much about those laws, but I knew Father was frequently opposing what were called "extensions" to licensing hours, and that it was an offense to sell drinks out of certain set hours. Only, it couldn't be all that late now.

"We only had soft drinks," I persisted as Mike remained grimly silent. "The police couldn't have made anything of that, could they? Perhaps they were looking for some criminal—"

"If you must know, they were after drugs."

"Drugs?"

"That's what Harry said. I guess there have been rumors that reefers and other forms of dope were being distributed there. Just my luck that the police chose tonight to raid the place!"

"Drugs?" I repeated, amazed. "But—you don't take drugs, Mike. You're not mixed up in that horrible mess."

"Of course not. I'm not that stupid," he said bluntly. "It wouldn't have been exactly pleasant though for our families to hear that we'd been questioned and possibly searched by the narcotics squad. But, thanks to Harry, the waiters will take it for granted that we had already left before the raid, and it's unlikely that anyone will mention our names."

"Unless the policeman got your license number."

"He didn't have a chance. Relax, now! We're in the clear."

I bit my lower lip hard. I supposed I should be grateful that he had whisked me away before the police had questioned us. Father would certainly have been horrified at my having been present during a police raid. Only, I was still angry with Mike for having taken me to that roadhouse at all, and I was still

14

shaken by our flight, and that incident with the policeman. I wasn't entirely satisfied by Mike's explanation either. I had an uneasy suspicion that there was more behind his action than he had revealed, because it wasn't like the daredevil Mike O'Donnell to panic.

He took a sharp corner at a fast speed, and I was flung half out of my seat.

"You're not relaxing," I protested. "Do you have to drive so fast?"

"The sooner we're safely back home, the better."

"Safely, yes," I said meaningfully.

"With hair like yours you shouldn't balk at a little speed!" he retorted with a grin which struck me as forced. "Don't worry!"

"If you drive at seventy through a restricted zone, you'll have the traffic cops after you," I said as we flashed past a thirty-mile-limit sign. "Do you want another ticket?"

"Oh, keep quiet! I can't stand backseat drivers."

We were rushing through a small suburb, approaching an intersection with red lights against us. Mike braked, but he had waited too long. The car skidded violently across the road and into the path of a large truck which was just coming off the side road. There was a sickening thud of crumpling metal, then the car seemed to rebound and swerve back to the left. Another, more violent impact—a horrible, rending sound— and I was flung forward against the dashboard. My head struck the windshield, and I must have blacked out for a minute or two.

I gasped out feebly, "Mike—Mike—" but there was no answer.

I grasped the steering wheel and pulled myself up. I could see Mike standing in the road with a gaunt, middle-aged, white-faced man who was shaking both fists at him. I supposed it was the truck driver.

"Now listen," Mike was saying urgently. "There's no need to bring the police into this. I'll pay for any damage."

"Nothing doing. Even though it might cost my job to report an accident, you asked for it. The lights were against you.

15

Young fools like you deserve to lose their licenses. Don't ask me to cover up for you!" the truck driver shouted at him.

"Charging across like a madman—"

"I'll make it worth your while—"

Their voices reached me as if from a great distance. My head felt as if it had been split in two by an ax, and the car seemed to be heaving around me. I knew I'd be sick if I moved—

Lights were flashing all around. I heard car engines and the sound of screeching brakes. There was a light in my eyes, blinding me.

"Are you hurt, dear?" That was a woman's voice. I tried to answer her but the words wouldn't come. Someone was çalling for an ambulance—

Then a girl's voice cried shrilly: "She's dead! Look at the blood! Get me out of this, Harry. Mike's really done it this time."

"Lucky for him that she was driving," a man's voice proclaimed. "It'll be hard on her old man though. Oh–oh, here comes a police car."

"*Dead?* Of course she's not dead. Come on, Lyra!" That was Mike's voice. He was leaning over me, speaking in a low, urgent tone. "Listen! Don't make a statement now if you feel too groggy. I'll explain that you didn't know the lights were there—that you braked hard and skidded. Just an error of judgment. They can't run you in for that."

It didn't make sense. He was talking as though I had been driving. Was he suffering from a concussion—or was I? He was hurling admonitions at me in that low, hurried tone, but I couldn't rouse myself to follow what he was saying. I felt too ill to care. Lights and voices and people—when all I wanted was to be left alone till this terrifying pain and dizziness passed.

Someone had me by the shoulders and was dragging me out of the car. The movement sent great waves of blackness rising up all around me. With a sudden fear that I was dying, I felt myself sinking down and down into the darkness.

16

2

"How COULD YOU DECEIVE US SO wantonly? Naturally, we thought you were at the concert. It was unforgiveable of you. How long has this been going on?"

"I'm sorry, Father," I said weakly. "How long has *what* been going on?"

"This deplorable liaison between you and Michael O'Donnell. When did it start?

The sun was streaming in through the window of the small white-walled hospital room. It hurt my eyes, and I blinked unhappily. Father was seated beside my bed, his gaunt, aquiline features looking as if they were carved out of granite, his pale blue eyes glittering at me frostily through his steel-rimmed glasses. He was pulling at his neatly trimmed gray beard; a familiar sign and the only one of mental perturbation I had ever known him betray. He might have been Moses calling down the wrath of God on the erring children of Israel. He was lashing me with words like hailstones. I put my hands up to my throbbing head. The bandages felt too tight—

"It wasn't like that," I protested feebly when he paused for breath. "I'd never been out with Mike before. Then it was only because of James. I mean, I didn't want to go to the concert alone. It was a mistake and—I've said I'm sorry."

"It's easy to say you're sorry, but actions speak louder than

17

words. Your professed penitence won't save us from the unpleasantness and publicity of police court proceedings," Father said harshly. "You'll be charged with careless if not with
dangerous driving. The police are waiting for a statement
from you as soon as Dr. Frencham says you're well enough to
talk to them."

"I'll be charged?" I said dazedly. "I can't be; I wasn't
driving."

Instead of looking relieved, his lips tightened and his glance
grew even more icy.

"It won't help to lie about it. There are several witnesses to
testify that you were in the driver's seat, slumped over the
wheel. Walter Mallard thinks your best course will be to plead
guilty and throw yourself on the judge's mercy. He wants to
see you before you make your statement."

"I'm not lying. I've never lied to you, Father," I answered
with a flash of hurt indignation. "Mike didn't even offer to let
me drive. I wouldn't have agreed anyway to drive an unfamiliar and powerful car like that at night."

"Are you expecting me to believe that all those witnesses
are prepared to give false evidence against you?" he said
incredulously.

"What witnesses?"

"Apart from young O'Donnell himself, Harry Grenley—
the accountant's son—and his fiancée, and two strangers who
were following the truck in their car, as well as the truck
driver," he said grimly. "It would be futile to try to convince
the police that they were all lying."

"Mike's lying," I said with a painful sense of betrayal. "The
others may be honestly mistaken. After the crash I tried to get
out, but I felt too dizzy. I guess I did collapse in the driver's
seat. I couldn't open the door on my side."

"Not a very plausible story, Lyra."

"It isn't a story. It's true. Why can't you believe me, Father?" I asked desperately. "I'm not in the habit of lying. Ask
Mother! She'll tell you."

"Unfortunately your poor mother is in no condition to
testify on your behalf," he said, his tone even grimmer. "She

18

was gravely worried when you didn't come home, and she answered the phone call from the police. The shock was too much for her; she collapsed with a heart attack."

"Mother? Mother's ill?" I faltered. "Where is she?"

"At home, in bed. The doctor says she must be kept absolutely quiet."

"Mother—" I couldn't remember that Mother had ever been ill, except with an occasional attack of flu. This was the worst blow of all. "I've got to get up and come home. If Mother's ill, she'll want me."

"You'll do nothing of the kind. You'll stay here until the doctor says you're well. Your aunt has her hands full enough looking after your mother; she can't be expected to nurse you too."

"I could help. Don't you understand? I want to be with Mother."

"I understand that you've done your mother enough damage already. She's had nothing but grief and anxiety from you," Father said coldly. "If my wishes meant little to you, one would have thought you might have shown some consideration for your mother's feelings before you gave her such a shock. You've made her really ill."

I swallowed a painful lump in my throat.

"I wouldn't have hurt Mother for the world," I said huskily. "Honestly, Father, the accident wasn't my fault. Mike was driving too fast, and I told him so. I see now that I shouldn't have gone out with him, but—"

"I don't want to listen to any excuses. Walter Mallard is prepared to undertake your defense. You'll do well to be guided by his advice," he interposed impatiently.

"You never listen to me—or to Mother either. I expect it was your reaction—your anger—which upset her," I blurted out impulsively. "The police must have told her that I wasn't badly hurt."

"You might have been killed. You've been unconscious for twenty-four hours. Worse, you might have killed someone else by your recklessness," he said sternly.

"Worse?" I echoed dully. "Yes, from your point of view,

19

that would have been worse, wouldn't it? You wouldn't have minded too much if I'd been killed. Why do you dislike me, Father?"

"You're talking nonsense. I've always done my duty toward you, but you've shown me singularly little gratitude and consideration in return," he said severely. "You've caused us endless trouble and expense and anxiety. Is it surprising that I find it difficult to believe in your contrition? To have your mother laid up now, with all the preparations for our bazaar next month in full swing, is most inconvenient. There's the Mother's Union social gathering next week, and we had offered to put up a preacher from the CPAS this coming weekend. I'll have to arrange for some other accommodation for him—"

My head was spinning as he reeled off a list of forthcoming engagements for which he had been counting on Mother's participation, and there was a painful ache in my heart. Was the inconvenience to his carefully organized plans more important to him than Mother's collapse and my accident? Didn't he realize—or didn't he care—that I was longing for some word of tenderness and reassurance?

The door opened to admit the serene-looking and comfortably plump head nurse. She glanced at me and then came over to the bed to adjust my pillows. One of them had slipped to the floor, but Father hadn't attempted to retrieve it.

"I must ask you to leave now, sir. Your daughter has talked enough," she pronounced crisply. "Dr. Frencham insisted that she shouldn't excite herself."

"I want to go home," I protested.

She shook her graying head at me. "Not just yet, dear. That was a bad gash you had on your head, and you were badly bruised and shocked."

Father rose, with a faint, chilly smile.

"You're in good hands, my child. I hope you'll do all you can to cooperate and give as little trouble as possible," he said austerely. "I shall pray for you—pray that you may have a change of heart and the grace to face up to the consequences of your wrongdoing."

I swallowed hard and gulped out, "Give my love to Mother, please." But he walked out without answering.

In his eyes, I am already judged and condemned, I thought bitterly. *Will the police and the judge take his view of the case? He said I'd have to plead guilty, but how can I?*

The nurse followed him out of the room. I had my face buried in the pillow and was crying helplessly when she came back.

"Now, now! This won't do. You'll make your head ache, and what have you to cry about, dear?" she said reprovingly. "You've had a merciful escape. You won't even have a scar to mar your pretty face."

"I wish I'd been killed," I said wildly. "My mother's ill from shock, and my father's furious with me. He won't believe that I wasn't responsible for the accident—"

"Don't worry about it now. Be thankful that it was no worse," she said kindly. "As I heard it, you didn't see the traffic lights until it was too late to stop for them."

"You heard that?" I jerked myself up on one elbow. "Who said so?"

"Young Mr. O'Donnell. He called to ask about you this morning. He was very concerned about you and anxious to see you, but the doctor said that only your family could be allowed to visit you today," she explained. "He's a charming young man, isn't he?"

"He's a liar," I said indignantly. "I wasn't driving his car; he was."

"You received a concussion, dear. Perhaps you've forgotten exactly what happened," she said soothingly.

"I haven't forgotten anything. Why would he say I was driving his car? It doesn't make sense."

"He couldn't have been driving. Don't you remember that court case last spring? It was his third offense and the judge suspended his license for a year. If he dares to drive without a license, he'll be in serious trouble."

I caught my breath sharply. So that was the answer! That was why Mike had refused to stop at the parking lot exit and show the policeman his license. He had taken a crazy chance

21

in driving out to the roadhouse, but he couldn't have anticipated that the police twenty miles from Kelchester would
demand to look at his license. No wonder he had panicked!
But surely he was man enough to take the consequences of his
law-breaking instead of trying to throw the blame on me? He
couldn't seriously expect me to lie on his behalf in the police
court.

"If he calls again, nurse, I would like to see him. Please, it's
urgent!" I said.

She smiled at me understandingly. "All right, dear. If the
doctor says you may." She nodded at a vase of exquisite
hothouse tea roses standing on the dresser. "Mr. O'Donnell
left those gorgeous roses for you. Did anyone tell you? Now
relax till we bring your tea, and no more tears, please. You
must remember that your father had a horrible shock, and
parents are always cross when they've been worried."

She trotted away and I lay back, trying to suppress the
burning tears which persisted in welling up in my eyes. Cross?
She imagined that Father was cross with me as a reaction from
his loving anxiety over his erring daughter!

If only it had been like that, I would be crying from sheer
relief, not from this unnerving sense of desolation.

He hadn't tried to reassure me about Mother's condition,
and he didn't want me to come home; he didn't really care
whether I lived or died. Why was it this way between us?
Surely he couldn't be jealous of the close ties between Mother
and me? Why did he believe the worst of me? I was his older
daughter. Couldn't he take my word?

My head was throbbing so painfully that it was difficult to
think. I tried to drink the tea that the nurse brought me, and
was promptly sick. After that everything grew hazy again until
I heard the murmur of voices beside my bed. I recognized the
nurse's and Dr. Frencham's. She was saying something about
my temperature and he was telling her that I was highly strung
and emotional and took after my mother.

"Mother—" I said desperately.

I forced my heavy eyelids back and clutched weakly at the
doctor's wrist. He was a big, bearlike man, with a gruff

manner but an innate kindliness which, as a child, I had intuitively recognized. I had never been afraid of Dr. Frencham.

"Hello. And how's my prettiest patient?" he asked, beaming down at me and patting my clinging fingers. "Still feeling under the weather?"

"Just worried. How is my mother, Dr. Frencham? Is she seriously ill?"

"Where did you get that idea? A few days in bed and she'll be herself again," he said in swift reassurance. "Of course, she's rundown. She's been overdoing with all these parish activities and a certain nervous strain."

"Father said I'd made her ill."

"I wouldn't put it quite like that. Her anxiety about you just brought things to a head. She has a slight heart strain, and she's at an age when a woman needs to take life easy and to avoid stress and strain. But there's no cause for alarm," he said kindly. "Now let's have a look at you. Silly young idiot, to bash yourself up like this, weren't you? You were lucky you didn't go through the windshield."

I felt my eyes beginning to fill with tears again, and he shook his head at me.

"Nothing to cry about, child. You aren't the first young person to be tempted into driving a powerful car too fast, and you certainly won't be the last. Be thankful no great damage was done," he admonished me, popping a thermometer into my mouth. "We'll give you something to make you sleep, and you'll feel a lot better tomorrow."

I wanted to protest that I hadn't been driving, but he held up his finger when I tried to speak. I had to wait until he had removed the thermometer and consulted it. Then he began to prepare an injection, and the nurse fussed around, straightening my pillows and rolling up my sleeve. Somehow it seemed too much of an effort to attempt to explain my story to Dr. Frencham. If my own father wouldn't believe it, why should he? Anyway, it didn't matter much what the doctor thought. It was whether the police believed me that mattered. If they didn't—

I was shivering as Dr. Frencham deftly shot the needle into my arm. I scarcely noticed the prick, and he patted my hand approvingly.

"That's a good girl! Now, stop fretting and let yourself drift. After a good night's sleep, your head will feel much better," he promised. "And don't worry about your mother. I'm keeping an eye on her, and your aunt is an excellent nurse."

His voice and everything in the room began to recede as the shot took effect. I was vaguely aware that the nurse was speaking to him and asking if it would be all right for me to see Mr. O'Donnell tomorrow, adding that she thought I would be less restless afterward.

"You're romantic, aren't you, nurse?" he chuckled. "Oh, well, I suppose the girl could do worse for herself! Nothing much wrong with that young man except high spirits and too much money, from all I've heard. He may slow down, given an incentive."

"He's terribly concerned about her. I had quite a job to keep him out today. They're obviously that way about each other," the nurse said sentimentally. "They must make a very handsome couple—"

I tried to call out, "You couldn't be more wrong—" but I was too drowsy.

Besides, I had to see Mike. He was the only person apart from myself who knew exactly what had happened. He had to tell the police the truth. He had to—

Dr. Frencham was right. I did feel better the next morning. My bruises still ached, but the painful throbbing in my head had subsided. The nurse assured me that my temperature was back to normal and, when a young nurse brought me a tempting breakfast tray, I discovered that I was hungry. She had barely taken away the tray before she was back again, beaming at me.

"Your boyfriend's here and waiting to see you, Miss Haughton. Boy, he's good-looking, isn't he? You're really lucky!" she said in naïve envy. "Do you want to do anything to your face before I bring him in?"

24

"No, thank you." I certainly didn't feel disposed to do anything for Mike's benefit.

My pulses quickened—with anger, not delight—as the nurse ushered him in. He was handsome enough to attract any woman's admiring glance, I couldn't deny that. Tall and dark, with boldly defined features and Irish blue eyes, he always looked and acted as if he were one of fortune's favorites.

"Lyra, my darling, how are you?" he exclaimed, striding across the small room with his most dazzling smile. "I've been awake all night worrying about you."

"That must have been a change," I said ironically. "I was under the impression that normally you worried only about your own precious skin."

"Now, don't be that way!" He sank into the chair beside my bed and reached for my hands, but I put them under the sheet hurriedly. "After all, I did my best to keep you in the clear. It was just bad luck that we had that accident."

"It was bad driving," I amended bluntly. "No thanks to you that we weren't killed."

His smile faded abruptly.

"Honestly, Lyra, I'm terribly sorry. I wouldn't have had you hurt for the world. You mean so much to me," he said earnestly. "I shouldn't have let you drive—"

"I wasn't driving. You can lie to everyone else, but it's useless for you to attempt to lie to me. I may have had a bad crack over the head but it hasn't affected my memory."

"Hasn't it? That's too bad! Don't you think it might? If you told the police that you couldn't remember anything about the accident, they'd probably let you off with a warning," he said persuasively.

"Unluckily for you, I remember only too well. How dare you try to wriggle out of the consequences at my expense?" I flashed. "Are you seriously expecting me to lie to the police for you?"

"No, my sweet. Merely to bend the truth a little. I'll make it up to you, I swear—and it's the easiest way out for both of us," he said meaningfully. "The judge will deal lightly with a first offense, if it does come to a court case. I'll really get it if they discover that I was driving with a suspended license. The insurance company won't pay for the damage either."

"You should have thought of that before you drove the car. You deserve all you'll get."

"Come now, is that a Christian attitude?" he asked reproachfully. "You're supposed to believe in loving your enemies and having compassion on them. Not that I'm your enemy—far from it—I'm your humble and devoted admirer. How can you talk in that harsh, merciless fashion? Are you really so unforgiving? Shame on you!"

"It isn't a question of forgiveness," I said wearily. "I can't go into the police court, take a solemn oath to speak the truth, and then lie."

His silky black brows drew together in an ominous frown.

"If you testify to what you imagine to be the truth, nobody will believe you. The judge will merely think you're trying to lie your way out of it. I've several reputable witnesses lined up who saw you in the driver's seat."

"Because I was struggling to get out of the car and my door was jammed. They'll have to believe me. And there must be people who saw *you* at the wheel," I said desperately. "Your friend Harry Grenley must have noticed you when you shot past his car at the exit of the parking lot."

"Harry won't breathe a word. He and his father consider my father one of their best clients."

"The truck driver—"

"I've taken care of him. He's absolutely convinced now that you were driving. It's no use; you can't win. You'll have to play it my way! In case you didn't know, money talks. So does my father's position," he said with emphasis. "Your father is anything but popular with the general public; nobody'll raise a finger to help his daughter. Think it over well before you stick out that pretty white neck of yours."

I almost hated him for having cornered me like this and for the cool cynicism with which he spoke. Yet—wasn't his whole behavior in character? He had been allowed to get away with too much in the past, through his personal charm, his father's money and his father's influence. It was natural for him to try

26

to take advantage now of all those assets, to use them to bring pressure to bear on me.

I was out on a limb—and on my own. I couldn't even turn to Mother for support. She was in no condition to be worried, so I couldn't involve her in any way. I had to make my own decision and see it through alone. The sickening part of it was that I knew Mike was right in saying that it would be easier for all concerned if I pretended that I had blacked out after the accident and let Walter Mallard enter a plea of guilty.

As if he had read my thoughts, Mike said triumphantly, "If you plead guilty, they won't question you, and you probably won't even have to go to court. Old man Mallard will represent you and talk judicially of extenuating circumstances, like the fact that you'd never handled a powerful sports car before, and were overexcited because you'd just become engaged. Everyone is sympathetic to a romance—even those tough old birds on the bench."

"Romance?" I echoed bitterly.

"Why not? Just say the word, and I'll announce our engagement. I'm head over heels in love with you, darling."

"A make-believe engagement, you mean? More lies," I said distastefully.

"No. No! The real thing. Can't you get it into your head that I want to marry you? I hadn't a chance while that plump young lawyer stuck to your side like glue. And, just when I was all ready to do the job properly, I have to rush you," he answered with what sounded like genuine regret. "You don't have to doubt that I'm in dead earnest though."

I felt quite dazed from shock. Mike O'Donnell, son of Kelchester's most prominent and wealthy citizen, the mayor, was actually proposing to me? Half the girls in the city were crazy about him and competing to catch him. Why in the world would he pick me?

"You don't love me," I said incredulously. "If you did, you wouldn't force me into this horrible situation."

"I've apologized for that, but frankly, you're taking it much too seriously. What's one traffic offense? If you're fined, my father will gladly pay. Leave the whole thing to Walter Mallard, and there'll be the minimum of unpleasantness," he said persuasively. "Don't hold it against me, darling, give me a break."

"You've got me all confused; I can't think straight. Our families—"

"Mine would be delighted. Father's perpetually nagging at me to find a nice girl and settle down. And wouldn't your father be pleased to have you off his hands?"

I flinched, and he want on swiftly, "It's common knowledge that your august father finds you a problem. You don't fit into his circle, but you would be a great success in ours. There's nothing my parents wouldn't do for us—"

Suddenly the door opened and the young nurse was smiling at us.

"Mr. Mallard is here, Miss Haughton. He says your father asked him to come," she announced.

"Then I'd better get going." Mike rose, and bent over to kiss me lightly on the cheek. "Think over what I've said, and don't decide anything in a hurry. I'll look in again tonight." Grinning, he turned to the wide-eyed nurse. "In the meantime, take care of my lovely girl for me!"

"Oh, I will!" she responded, but her eyes were fixed on him, not on me.

3

"THAT'S WHAT YOU THINK HAPPENED, but isn't it possible that you're still a little confused after your concussion?" Walter Mallard suggested.

I drew a quick, impatient breath. He had heard me out with scarcely a comment, but apparently he didn't believe me.

He was a short, stout man with graying, wispy hair and a florid complexion. I had long ago recognized the family resemblance between him and James, but not until Mike had spoken of "that plump young lawyer" had I realized that, when he was middle-aged, James might be a replica of his father—overweight, balding and maddeningly deliberate in his speech and movements.

"What you mean is that you would like me to plead guilty," I said bitterly, "even though I'm not?"

His sparse, gray brows drew together. He gave me a long considering glance.

"The evidence is all against you," he pointed out judicially. "The judge will obviously be reluctant to accept your unsupported word. It will be much worse for your father to have his daughter branded a liar than to have her fined for careless driving. Shouldn't you consider his feelings and your mother's too?"

"Not to mention Mike O'Donnell's and the mayor's."

"Precisely. Mr. O'Donnell is very generous. He insisted on

this private room for you and he has also volunteered to pay our fees for representing you."

"Expense is no object—provided that he can keep his adored son out of the police court? If I tell the truth and the judge believes me, Mike will be in real trouble, won't he?" I challenged him.

"Undoubtedly. *If*—" he emphasized gravely. "I'm sure you wouldn't want that, especially when you can't possibly be sure of what happened after such a bad crack on the head."

"I wish I weren't," I said unhappily. "Honestly, Mr. Mallard, I'm only too clear about it. I was begging Mike not to drive so fast in a residential district. Then I saw the red lights—"

He frowned in a baffled fashion. "Naturally, if you're convinced of that, I can't advise you to plead guilty," he said with patent reluctance. "But remember, you'll be under oath."

"That's the whole point," I said wearily. "I certainly have no desire to get Mike into trouble, but how can I swear to tell the truth and then lie?"

"Well, there's no need to decide upon your course of action just yet. There won't be any charge brought against you while you're in the hospital. Apart from your injuries, Dr. Frencham says you're still in shock," he said hastily. "If your father hadn't made a point of it, I wouldn't have worried you about the legal aspect just yet. We'll have another talk when you're better."

He heaved himself out of the chair as if eager to escape.

"We miss you in the office," he added with a forced smile. "James sent you his best wishes for a swift recovery. Take things easy now."

"None of this would have happened if James had taken me to the concert," I said impulsively. "Why did you tell him to see less of me, Mr. Mallard? What do you have against me?"

"Nothing, my dear. Nothing at all. I simply think it's a mistake for a young man at the start of his professional career to become involved with any one particular girl."

That came out much too smoothly, as though he had formu-

30

lated it against such a question, I thought resentfully. *It's virtually word for word the excuse James gave me. It's plausible, but hardly convincing. James and I have been close friends for years. Why should his father urge him to draw back now?*

Before I could find the courage to press him for a more revealing answer, he had given me another meaningless smile and left. I stared forlornly at the gorgeous roses on the dresser.

Money talks. I had heard that phrase often enough but had never realized its significance before. Even Walter Mallard, whom I had always regarded as a lawyer of integrity, had listened to the voice of money and power. Presumably James had too, and that was why he had sent me a message instead of coming to see me.

James surely knew me too well to doubt my word, but it seemed that he was reluctant to involve himself by taking my side. Evidently he intended to watch from the sidelines. It was a bitter, disillusioning thought. Wasn't there anyone who would urge me to listen to the "still small voice" of my own conscience? What about Aunt Clara? "Tell the truth and shame the devil" was one of her pet mottoes. It was her excuse for what she called "plain speaking"—speaking which I had often considered unnecessarily unkind. What about my sister, Dorothea? Wasn't she always "on the side of the angels"?

It was a long morning. I wished that I was in a double room. Shut away there with nothing to do except think, I felt terribly isolated. I hoped that Dorothea would come to see me during her lunch hour, but she didn't. I wondered if she took Father's view of the whole mess. It was sad to reflect how little warmth and sympathy and affection existed between my sister and myself. In our childhood I had tried to mother and protect her, but even as a toddler she had been oddly self-sufficient.

"Such a good little girl," Aunt Clara had said fondly about her. I couldn't remember that Dorothea had ever been messy or untidy, hurt or in tears, needing any comfort or support from me.

In our school days, the three years' difference between our ages had prevented us from seeing a great deal of each other.

31

Our tastes had been entirely different too—as different as our school careers. Mine had been a series of ups and downs. Dorothea had plodded through hers. At nineteen she had been accepted at the Kelchester Church of England Training College for Teachers, where she was now a second-year student. She had never shown any flashes of brilliance, but she had worked hard. She hadn't made many friends, but she hadn't made any enemies either. Ever since she was little she had worn glasses for shortsightedness, so she hadn't done well in sports; and she had considered extracurricular activities a waste of time.

I had been on the tennis and lacrosse teams and had belonged to the school's choral and debating societies, the nature study club, and the musical appreciation club. My grades were as high as Dorothea's, yet, somehow, Father and Aunt Clara hadn't considered my school record as "satisfactory" as my sister's. Aunt Clara had been prone to complain tartly that I was too fond of making myself conspicuous.

If Mother wasn't seriously ill, Dorothea would be at college as usual, I supposed, but she could have spared a few minutes during her lunch hour to visit me. The college was less than a five-minute walk from Victoria Hospital. She must have known that I would be eager for the latest news of Mother.

Instead, my next visitor was Mary Mallard, James' sister. She arrived at teatime, flushed and breathless, and dropped a sheaf of magazines and a box of peppermint creams on my bed.

"Sorry I couldn't make it before, but we've had a rush all day," she explained apologetically.

Mary worked as a librarian in the county library. She had been one of my best friends at school and I was unfeignedly glad to see her. At one time we had gone around together constantly; but since she had become engaged to a young schoolteacher, she had had less time to spare for me.

She flopped into the chair beside my bed, pushed back her fair curls from her flushed forehead, and tugged her short skirt down over her plump knees.

"Did you know you're the talk of Kelchester?" she rushed

32

on with her habitual volubleness. "Everyone's hinting that there's something between you and Mike O'Donnell. The girls are wild with envy. True—or false?"

"If it were true, would *you* envy me?" I challenged her.

"Well, no! Apart from the fact that I have George, Mike isn't my type," she answered with her characteristic candor. "Of course, he's an awfully good catch, but I always thought that you and James—"

She broke off abruptly, her color deepening.

"So did I. And I was sure he did too," I said ruefully. "Why has James suddenly changed toward me, Mary? Do you know?"

"Not really. I overheard part of a conversation he was having with Dad about you, but I didn't hear enough to make sense." She looked embarrassed—a rare state for Mary, who was always frank and open and unself-conscious. "Dad's been making a new will for your father—or so I gathered. I believe it has something to do with that."

"With my father's will?" I said incredulously. "How could that possibly concern James?"

She wriggled uncomfortably, and light dawned on me.

"Oh! You mean that my father hasn't left me any money? But, why should he leave me any? Naturally he'll leave everything to Mother," I said perplexedly. "Anyway, Father's only in his fifties—"

"Of course. And he'll probably live to a ripe old age," she said hurriedly. "I don't think it's that exactly. James isn't especially mercenary, and I'm sure he thinks a lot of you."

"Then why did he date my sister instead of me?"

"Search me! I asked him about it, but he was deliberately evasive." She wrinkled up her nose. "Don't worry! I'll get to the bottom of it eventually. Tell me about what happened with Mike—"

I told her the whole story. Mary was one of the few people I trusted unreservedly. Without being in the least priggish or pious or bigoted, she was truly good, with a live and shining faith. Her parents and brothers were regular churchgoers, but

Mary's belief went much deeper than mere conventional acceptance. It was something real and personal.

She heard me out in silence, then said impulsively, "Oh, how terrible for you! I'm *so* sorry. Only, of course, you'll have to tell the truth just as you remember it. You'd always have it on your conscience if you didn't."

"That's how I feel," I said, warmly grateful for her understanding. "But—they've left me all confused. They seem to think it would be deplorably selfish and un-Christian of me to give Mike away. And, with his witnesses against me, it will be tougher on Father too. Your father and mine want to hush the whole thing up—and keep me out of court if possible. They believe the judge will let me off lightly in view of the extenuating circumstances. I suppose that's why Mike has started that rumor circulating."

"Probably, though I do think he's really sold on you. I've noticed the way he looks at you on the rare occasions when he comes to St. Saviour's with his parents—and at parties too. You never appeared to be aware of him, and I suppose he took that as a challenge," she said reflectively. "Is your father worldly minded enough to want you to marry Mike?"

"Oh, I doubt it!" I said hastily. "I sincerely hope not. I haven't seen Father since Mike proposed to me this morning, but he wouldn't urge me to marry a man I barely know, would he? Besides, I'm sure he doesn't approve of Mike. How could he?"

"I suppose he might see Mike as a 'brand to be snatched from the burning.' It would be a dangerous operation though. You would probably end up getting badly burned," Mary said humorously. "I can't picture you in the role of missionary; you're too emotional and not tough enough."

"What you mean is that I'm not a good enough Christian."

"I didn't say that and I didn't think it. We don't all have the same gifts. You can't preach and you haven't the patience to be a teacher. Your kind of witness is in your life. You ran 'the straight race' at school all right and you were a 'good neighbor' too. You influenced people without consciously trying,"

34

she said kindly. "Mike would be too hard a nut for you to crack though. Don't try!"

"If I give him away to the police, I'm not likely to have the chance. He'll be furious with me."

"Perhaps—" She shook back her curls, putting her head on one side meditatively. "Perhaps he'll admire you all the more for sticking to your guns."

"The worst part of it is that everyone will think I'm trying to clear myself by throwing Mike to the wolves," I said miserably.

"I know. I see that. It would be much easier for you to accept the blame," Mary said sympathetically. "It'll be a tough test, but Christ never promised that we would find it smooth sailing to follow Him. By resisting all the pressure and standing by the truth, you'll be witnessing in a very real way."

"Shall I? If nobody believes me—"

"Yes, even then," she said steadily. "Try not to worry. The truth is bound to come to light eventually, and in the long run that'll be better for Mike himself. He needs a sharp jolt—needs to realize that he can't go through life dodging consequences. This might be the turning point for him. It would really be wonderful if you were the means of winning him for Christ."

"You're so much braver than I am," I sighed.

"Not by nature. It's just that when I'm up against anything, I remind myself that 'I can do all things through Christ which strengtheneth me.' The strength is always there," she said quietly. "We only have to reach out for it. I'll pray for you. and I'll talk with Dad too."

That was so typical of Mary that I smiled. Not only would she pray for anyone in trouble, but she would also do everything she could to help. She was essentially a practical as well as a practicing Christian.

Only, there weren't so many stumbling blocks in Mary's path, I thought wistfully after she had gone. Her fiancé shared her faith. At present he was helping to support a widowed mother and educate younger brothers and sisters, but he was hoping to go abroad some day and teach in a mission school, and Mary was eagerly looking forward to that. In the meantime, she was happy in her work, and she had a happy home-life too.

I wondered again if it was my fault that I seemed to be such a misfit at home. Not entirely, I was sure. How could I love Father and Aunt Clara as I should when they showed me so little affection?

Aunt Clara came stalking into my room later that evening, tall and gaunt in her overly long, unbecoming gray suit, a mushroom-shaped hat in a different shade of gray crammed uncompromisingly on her iron-gray hair, her lips compressed, her pale blue eyes frosty.

"Well, how are you? Ashamed of yourself, I hope!" she greeted me. "Worrying your poor mother, and causing all this commotion!"

"How is Mother?" I asked urgently.

"Naturally she's greatly distressed on your account, and on your father's." She added in a grudging tone, "She sent you her love and said she hoped you would soon be home again. Really, I can't see why the doctor's keeping you here. You don't look as if there's much wrong with you. You certainly don't need a private room, a most unnecessary expense."

"I was told that it was Mr. O'Donnell's idea, and that he's paying for it."

She seated herself squarely on the bedside chair and scrutinized me severely.

"Oh, was it? Are you telling me that there's some truth in the rumor that young O'Donnell is fond of you?"

"I don't know. Mike has asked me to let him announce our engagement, but we're almost strangers."

"Trust you to land on your feet!" she said acidly. "You and that wild Irishman will make a good pair. Well, at least you'll be off your unfortunate father's hands."

I blinked at her incredulously. "Aunt Clara, you sound as if you want me to marry Mike. I couldn't possibly marry him."

"Can't? Nonsense! What else can you do after getting yourself involved with him? You're lucky to have the chance. The announcement will silence most of the gossip and be a weight off your poor father's mind," she retorted decisively. "You've always been an anxiety to him. Once you're safely married, you'll be the O'Donnells' responsibility, not his."

I felt as though she had slapped me across the face. Did she have to talk as if I were a problem child, or a ne'er-do-well, of whom my parents were yearning to wash their hands? The injustice of that stung me badly. I was used to her chilly disapproval, but I had never been quite so acutely aware of her hostility toward me.

"I don't understand you, Aunt Clara," I said, struggling to keep my tone even. "As a professing Christian, how can you urge your niece to marry a man who doesn't believe in anything except pleasing himself?"

"You're no niece of mine," she snapped. "Your parents have done their duty by you, and so have I, but it's high time you ceased making demands on us and usurping Dorothea's position. If you've a chance to marry, I strongly advise you to take it before you get yourself in worse trouble and humiliate all of us."

"I don't know what you mean," I said in bewilderment. "I've usurped Dorothea's position? How?"

There was a brief tense pause. She was sitting bolt upright, her hands clasped around her serviceable brown handbag, her feet in their heavy, sensible black walking shoes planted firmly on the floor. Her pale blue eyes narrowed as she surveyed me. A faint flush stained her sallow cheeks.

Then, as if bracing herself, she lifted her square chin and said, with just a flicker of compunction, "I've argued this question with your mother for many years. She can be very stubborn, and she has persistently refused to tell you the facts. I've respected her wishes, but you've gone too far now. I fail to see why my brother should suffer simply because she has this dread of hurting you. In my candid opinion, you've forfeited all right to her consideration by this last escapade of yours."

"I'm still in the dark. What are you hinting at, Aunt Clara?" I asked apprehensively. "Facts?"

"Yes. You're a big girl now, and a tiresome, headstrong

girl, as might have been expected. Blood always tells," she said, her tone hardening again. "No daughter of my brother's could have behaved as you have. It's obvious that you must be your real mother over again."

"My—my real mother?" I faltered.

"Yes. You're an adopted child, Lyra. Didn't that ever occur to you?"

"No. No, of course not," I gasped. "You mean that Father isn't my father? And Mother? She isn't my mother? Oh, I can't believe that! We've been so close to each other—Mother and I."

It was a shattering shock. The white walls seemed to be swaying around me. As if through a mist, I was conscious of Aunt Clara's cold, implacable scrutiny, and of her stern voice as she admonished me to pull myself together. She wouldn't lie to me; I realized that with sickening force. Monstrous, incredible and painful as her bald statement appeared to me, I couldn't refute it.

"I was adopted," I said dazedly. "When? And—and who am I? Who were my real parents?"

"We've never known. You were about four months old when your mother found you on the vicarage porch on Christmas Eve. That was in Devon, where my brother had a country parish at the time. Your mother had just lost her own first baby and there were fears that she could never have another," Aunt Clara said calmly. "That was the only reason why, after all inquiries failed to trace your parents, my brother consented to adopt you. Your mother was convinced that you had been sent to her as a Christmas gift."

"From Saint Nicholas?"

"Precisely. She would have named you after him, but you had already been christened Lyra. Such a preposterous name! Did you really imagine that my brother would have christened a daughter of his Lyra?"

"Mother told me that I was named after a star, because that constellation—Lyra—was shining brilliantly on the night I was born," I said dully. "Lyra means 'The Harp.' Mother said

38

it was appropriate, but I often wondered how she could have foreseen that music would mean so much to me."

"Obviously it was in your blood," Aunt Clara retorted, as if music were some form of inherited disease. "No doubt your parents were penniless musicians who didn't want to be bothered with a baby."

I drew a long, painful breath. I could dimly perceive the picture now and could understand why Father had always been so severe with me. He had agreed to adopt me for Mother's sake, but he had never really wanted me or taken me to his heart. Aunt Clara had felt the same way. After my sister's birth both of them had resented my being treated as the older daughter. My sister? Dorothea wasn't my sister; there was no blood tie between us.

It was a shock to realize that. And yet, it was something of a relief. For years I had felt guilty because I couldn't get close to Dorothea. Now I understood why, and it no longer seemed strange that we had so little in common. It drew the sting out of Aunt Clara's disapproval too. It explained why she had regarded me with such suspicion and prejudice, why all her affection had been lavished on Dorothea.

"Why have you told me now?" I asked suddenly.

Being basically honest, she didn't attempt to prevaricate.

"For all our sakes. You've been a cause of dissension between your foster parents for many years. It's essential that your mother shouldn't be worried now. If you've any genuine affection for her and, to be fair to you, I believe you do, you must cease to make emotional demands on her," she said crisply. "Leave her to her husband and her own daughter."

"Leave her? Leave Mother?" A lump rose in my throat, making it difficult to speak. "I can't. I love her. I couldn't love her more if she were my own mother."

"Then you should consider her feelings and stop clinging to her. It's time the cuckoo in the nest spread her wings. You're no fledgling now, Lyra," she said relentlessly.

"How?"

She shrugged her shoulders.

"That's up to you. If you don't wish to marry young O'Donnell, you can find yourself another job, away from Kelchester. Walter Mallard says you're a competent secretary."

"Does he know? Does James?" I asked painfully. "Who else?"

"Nobody here. It has been a closely guarded secret. Your father didn't tell Walter Mallard until quite recently."

"When he made his will?" I asked, remembering what Mary had said. "I suppose he felt he had to explain why he wasn't making any provision for me. And—and Mr. Mallard told James. That was why James suddenly decided to drop me."

"That young man has a good head on him. Naturally he wouldn't care to involve himself with a girl of unknown and probably undesirable parentage. The Mallards are highly respected here." Aunt Clara eyed me with a kind of grudging pity. "There's no need to look so stricken. A lawyer has to be careful of his reputation. It's different for young O'Donnell. In any case, he doesn't have to know."

"You think I could marry Mike without telling him? I have *some* standards, Aunt Clara. I couldn't consciously deceive anyone, as you've all conspired to deceive me," I said bitterly. "Why wasn't I told about this years ago?"

"Mistaken kindness on your mother's part. Poor Anne didn't realize what she was doing. I tried to warn her, but she wouldn't listen."

4

"MUMMIE—OH, DARLING MUMMIE—" I stroked the slender
fingers which were quivering in mine. "Don't cry. Please! I
didn't mean to hurt you."

"You've always been like my own baby to me. I was sure
you were sent to me by God to take the place of the baby I'd
lost," Mother said forlornly. "You've given me so much happiness—and now— Oh, why did Clara have to interfere?"

Teardrops were trembling on her brown eyelashes. Her
delicately shaped lips twisted. Lying propped up on a mound
of pillows in the big double bed, she looked very small and
defenseless. I had a sudden feeling that we had changed
places. Ever since I could remember, she had been shielding
me and taking my side. Now it was my turn to protect and
reassure her. I couldn't add to her distress by reproaching her
for having kept the facts about my real parents from me. She
had acted from the best possible motives. In her love and
tenderness toward me, she had hoped that I would never need
to know that I had been an unwanted, abandoned baby.

"I suppose Aunt Clara thought she was doing the right
thing," I conceded reluctantly. "For Father's sake, anyway."

A tremor shook her and she clasped my hand more tightly.
She was much too loyal and devoted a wife to ever criticize
Father to me, but she must know much better than I did that
he had regretted adopting me.

"What should I do?" I asked desperately. "Shall I play along with them and marry Mike?"

"Not unless you love him, darling. Marriage isn't always easy for a woman. Men can be very difficult at times. Only a deep abiding love can give a wife patience, tolerance and understanding," she answered, as if from her heart. "Love and a shared faith are essential. 'Can two walk together, except they be agreed?' Perhaps I don't know the O'Donnells well enough to be able to advise you but, if Mike is urging you to lie on his behalf, he can't be the kind of man I would choose for my beloved child."

A lump rose in my throat. "You still feel like that about me, Mummie? That I'm your child?"

"Of course, my darling," she said fondly. "Always. You were sent to me. My faith and courage were at a very low ebb after I lost our first baby. Then you came and took all the bitterness away. I told myself that there was some good reason, hidden from us, why I'd had to endure that dreadful grief and then had been given you to take my baby's place. It was God's plan for us—"

"A plan which couldn't have been easy for you," I said compassionately. "Father—"

I checked myself as her delicate, blue-veined eyelids fluttered. I didn't want to distress her by letting her know that I had guessed years ago that Father had no love to spare for me.

"Your father doubted the wisdom of adopting a baby whose parents we couldn't trace," she said slowly. "I persuaded him that we must accept you as a gift from God. It was the first time I had ever withstood Herbert. Perhaps that was part of the pattern too. I was so much in love with him that I was all too easily submerged, and tended to let him make every decision for us both. I had to learn that there were times when I must think and act for myself."

"Then you haven't any regrets?"

"None at all," she answered unhesitatingly. "You've been a great comfort to me, darling. Perhaps I should have told you the facts before this, but I wasn't brave enough. I was afraid of hurting you and spoiling things for you. Try to understand!"

"I do understand. Don't worry about it," I said quickly, as her voice quivered.

I thought I knew how she had felt. We had always had such a close and loving relationship. In a very real way I had been hers—all hers—as Dorothea hadn't. From early childhood Dorothea had been "Daddy's girl." She hadn't appreciated Mother's gentle, sensitive, unselfish nature as I had, and she had never needed the tenderness which Mother had lavished on me. Only, as Aunt Clara had pointed out, I wasn't a fledgling now. For Mother's own sake I couldn't go on clinging to her. I had to spread my wings. If I stayed at home, Mother would inevitably be involved in endless controversy about Mike and the forthcoming court case. She would be torn by conflicting loyalties. I had to spare her that. She had accepted my version unquestioningly, but I knew Father and Aunt Clara wouldn't or couldn't believe that I was telling the truth; they were firmly convinced that there was "bad blood" in me and that it was showing itself now.

I had been too dazed by the shock of Aunt Clara's revelation to think much about my unknown parents. Suddenly curiosity stirred in me. What kind of people had they been to deposit a helpless baby on someone else's doorstep? Utterly heartless and irresponsible? Or had there been some vital reason why they couldn't keep me?

As if she had followed my trend of thought, Mother said gently, "Don't ever imagine that you were ever unloved or unwanted, Lyra. Your mother surrendered you for your own sake."

"How do you know? You didn't know her, did you? Aunt Clara said you tried to trace her and failed."

"I couldn't be sure. So many expectant mothers and mothers with young children were evacuated to country districts in those horrible war years. We had our quota at St. Cyriac's. I do know that she had been among our congregation because she said so in the note she left pinned to your little coat. You were beautifully dressed, and wrapped in a fleecy, hand-knitted shawl—"

"There was a note? What did it say?" I asked eagerly. "Do you still have it?"

"No. Your father gave it to the police. I can remember it almost word for word though. Your mother wrote that your father had been killed in an air raid while acting as a part-time air-raid warden, and she believed that she was soon to join him. She had to go into the hospital for a major operation, and she had been warned that she had only a slight chance of surviving it. She had no fear for herself, but she dreaded the thought of leaving her baby to be reared in an orphanage. Her one wish for you was that you should be brought up in a Christian home, in the faith which had sustained your parents."

"Oh!" I said, startled. "That doesn't sound as if they had been what Aunt Clara called 'undesirable characters.'"

"I'm sure they weren't," Mother said firmly. "Your aunt imagined that the note was a calculated appeal to my credulity, but I never doubted your mother's sincerity. She said that she had seen me in church and heard of the sad loss I had suffered. She begged me to take you to my heart in the place of the child who had been stillborn. She promised that if she pulled through the operation, she would get in touch with me. But evidently she didn't because I never heard from her again."

"Was that all? She didn't give you her name?"

"No. Only your Christian name and the reason she had chosen it."

"Then I shall never know who she and my father were," I said disappointedly. "If you couldn't trace her at the time, it would be hopeless to try now."

There was a sudden silence between us. Mother's color had risen faintly and her lips were quivering.

"Does it matter to you?" she asked at last, a look of reproach in her velvet brown eyes. "Isn't it enough that you're our dearly loved daughter? Do you really want to probe into that distant past?"

"Yes, I do, because it's terrible not to know the whole truth about it. People like Aunt Clara will always believe the worst

44

of my parents. Mike says he doesn't care who or what they were, but the Mallards care. James shied away from me as soon as he learned that I was an adopted child," I answered candidly. "Besides, though I know you love me, Mummie, I'm not Father's 'dearly loved daughter.' I never have been, and it would be a relief to him if I were to go away."

She couldn't refute that. Tears filled her eyes again.

"Then I'll have to give you the note. I hoped I never would need to, but you must not marry Mike O'Donnell just to get away from home," she said tremulously.

"Note?" I echoed sharply.

"The sealed envelope your mother left with me. It was marked 'For my daughter when she is twenty-one.' Even your father doesn't know of its existence, because he would have insisted upon opening it. I couldn't, though often I longed to, because I felt your mother had trusted me to keep it for you. It came by mail on New Year's Day, with no covering letter, but a London postmark on the outer envelope. I suppose she was in a London hospital when she wrote it."

"You've kept it a secret all these years? Why didn't you give it to me when I was twenty-one?"

"You seemed to be settling down happily in Walter Mallard's office, and I hoped you were going to marry James. How could I suddenly spring the facts about your adoption on you?" she countered. "I was sorely tempted to destroy that sealed letter, unread. Try to understand, darling. I thought of you as my daughter. Perhaps it was wrong and selfish of me, but I didn't want to share you with a ghost from the past."

I nodded. I could appreciate her feeling of maternal possession, but hadn't I a right to this one message from my real mother? Wasn't it natural that I should yearn to know something of her? Especially if it hadn't been through irresponsibility that she had given me to strangers.

"Where is it? Please, Mummie, let me have it," I said urgently.

"It's locked in the bottom of that old cashbox of my mother's, Lyra darling. Are you sure you want to read it?"

Ordinarily I could never harden my heart against that look

of pleading in her eloquent eyes. I sensed that she was willing me to say that the past wasn't important, that she was my mother—the only mother that I could ever love or need. But, the past couldn't be obliterated now that I was aware of it, and I had to find out all I could about my unknown parents. Not simply for my own peace of mind, but also for the sake of any man who might want to marry me.

Yet, when at last I held that small white envelope with its faded inscription, I discovered that my hands were trembling. Perhaps I dimly perceived even then that to open it might be to change the whole course of my life. But how could I not read this final—this only—letter from the woman who had brought me into the world? Mother must have realized that, or she wouldn't have kept the envelope safely locked away all these years. She sighed deeply, and then the bedroom door swung open.

With a swift, instinctively defensive movement, I thrust the envelope into the pocket of my tweed suit and turned to meet Aunt Clara's disapproving gaze.

"You've talked long enough. I warned you not to tire your mother; now she looks exhausted," Aunt Clara said coldly.

She crossed to the bed and plumped up Mother's pillows. Then she smoothed back Mother's brown hair as if tending a child. She had always treated Mother as her much younger sister, to be alternately dominated and protected.

"Time for your pills, Anne," she said in a gentler tone. "Then you must rest before supper. I've a lovely fresh Dover sole for you. I'm cooking it in milk so that it'll be easy to digest."

As she turned to the bedside table to get the pills, Mother and I exchanged glances. Mother's faint smile made me ashamed of my irritation at the interruption. She could accept Aunt Clara's actions in the spirit in which they were intended. I knew, too, that Aunt Clara was sincerely fond of Mother and meant to be kind, but I found it difficult to tolerate her high-handed ways.

"I'll see you later, darling," Mother murmured.

I nodded and almost ran from the room. I had an absurd

fear that Aunt Clara's penetrating gaze might spot the precious envelope in my pocket; and she was the last person with whom I would want to share its contents. I hurried down the corridor to my own small bedroom, and locked the door after me.

Suddenly weak at the knees, I sank down on my bed. Dr. Frencham had not really wanted to let me leave the hospital that afternoon, but I had persuaded him that the enforced inactivity, with nothing to do except think, was becoming unendurable. Also, I didn't want to accept any more from the O'Donnells.

With shaking fingers, I ripped open the envelope and drew out three sheets of paper. With dawning excitement, I saw that two of them were documents—a marriage license and a birth certificate. So, at any rate, my mother had been legally married to my father, I thought in swift relief, and in church too. It gave me the strangest feeling to stare at those two totally unfamiliar names—David Amberton and Grace Margaret Trevinion—and to realize that they were the names of my real parents. I read the birth certificate again. It was like suddenly being given a new identity to see that I had been registered as Lyra Grace Amberton.

So I had been christened after my unknown mother too? Perhaps Father would have liked me better if I had been named Grace instead of Lyra, I reflected. Grace was a beautiful name. A pang of loss shot through me that I would never now see the owner of it who had been my mother.

Her letter was headed with the address of a well-known London hospital. The writing was pitiably shaky, as if she had been almost too weak to hold a pen.

MY DARLING LITTLE LYRA,

When you read this, I shall be with your father, who entered into the joy of our Lord a month before you were born. He died as he had lived, working to save others. He was killed while helping to rescue survivors from a bombed air-raid shelter. He was a curate in the city church where we were married. I wish I could tell you about him

47

and how proud and happy I am to have been his wife, but I am very weak tonight.

I hope and pray that I have chosen the right foster parents for my baby. Anne Haughton has a sweet and loving expression. I believe she will love you and care for you as if you were her own, and bring you up in the faith which inspired your dear father and has sustained me ever since I met him. It gave me the courage to withstand my parents' plans for me and to marry your father.

Mine wasn't a Christian home, and I never knew real happiness and peace of mind till the mission in which your father was taking part led me to Christ. That is why I haven't told my family of your birth or asked them to take you. They would be good to you in their own fashion, but they know nothing of the "unsearchable riches"—the only riches I want my child to value.

When you read this, though, you will be old enough to make decisions for yourself; and if you are like your father you won't be influenced by worldly considerations. You may feel a desire to visit your relatives at The Manor, Trevinion, near Port Petroc. I leave that to you.

The nurse is coming to turn out the lights, so I must say good night and God bless you, my darling baby.

Your loving,
MOTHER

For a moment, tears blurred my eyes—tears for that young widow, far from her home and family, who had given her baby to strangers, and had lain dying in a big, impersonal city hospital. I could pity her from my heart, but her letter had stirred resentment in me too. Why had she left me on the vicarage porch as if I were a foundling, the unwanted child of an unmarried couple? Why, if she had had a home and parents, had she arbitrarily cut me off from them? She couldn't have been sure that the vicar and his wife would adopt me; they might have sent me to an orphanage. Surely her own family would have been the right people to care for me. It wasn't as though they had been in dire financial straits. From their address, and what she had written about "riches," they must have been well-to-do. There had been no need for

48

me to be brought up as a charity child, or to be adopted and eyed askance by my foster father and his sister.

It was as if my mother had deliberately robbed me of my birthright, I thought rebelliously. I ought to have been with the Trevinions or the Ambertons. Surely they would have welcomed me for my parents' sake.

"Mine wasn't a Christian home. . . ." Wasn't that an unnecessarily harsh judgment? Obviously Grace Trevinion had had a disagreement with her parents in her determination to marry David Amberton. Probably they hadn't wanted her to become the wife of a penniless clergyman, but did that mean that they were pagans? They might have given me that sense of security and belonging and affection which Father and Aunt Clara hadn't. They would have been my own kin—

There was a tap on the door.

"Who is it?" I called defensively.

"Mary. I was told at the hospital that you'd come home." The door handle turned. Then she asked on a note of apprehension, "Why have you locked the door? Are you all right? Shall I go away?"

"No. Come in, if you like—"

I got up to unlock the door. I felt completely confused; I had to talk to someone, and Mary was always a safe confidante. I could trust her and could rely on her sound common sense. She would be able to appraise Grace Margaret Trevinion's letter without the mixed, churned-up emotions which were devastating me.

I poured the whole story into Mary's receptive, sympathetic ears, and then handed her the documents.

"I can't think of Grace Margaret Trevinion as 'Mother.' She disowned me; she deliberately cut me off from her own family," I said resentfully. "Why? Do you suppose her illness clouded her brain? Or was she some kind of religious fanatic?"

"She was young—only twenty-one when she married your father and twenty-two when you were born—" As usual, Mary had seized on the concrete facts. "She must have sensed that she was going to die, and her one idea was to safeguard her baby."

"By handing me over to strangers?"

"If she had been attending your father's church and seen your mother there, she probably felt that she knew them quite well and could trust them," Mary said thoughtfully. "It must have been a terribly difficult decision for her to make, with nobody to advise her. As I see it, her parents hadn't welcomed her conversion or her marriage. I imagine that they had tried to pressure her into marrying some wealthy, worldly type like Mike O'Donnell, and that wasn't at all what she wanted for her daughter. She was relying on the Haughtons to give you her own sense of values."

"Father and Aunt Clara's?" I said bitterly.

"Don't forget that your father was a lot younger in those days, and he hadn't been married long. He would have been less unyielding and more sympathetic. He probably reminded her of David Amberton," Mary said sagely. "She was right about Anne Haughton, anyway. No mother could have cared more for you. Can you regret having been brought up by her?"

I shook my head confusedly.

"She has been a wonderful mother to me, of course. Only, I've never really belonged to her as I would have belonged to my own mother's people. Oh, Mary, I'm all mixed up, and feeling as though I've been cheated!"

"That's a natural reaction," she answered calmly. "Especially just now when you've been badly hurt by the archdeacon's refusal to take your word about that accident. Don't jump to conclusions though. Without having met the Trevinions, you can't possibly guess what kind of a life you would have led with them at Port Petroc."

"The manor house sounds as if they were well to do."

"Perhaps, but is money important to you, Lyra? I wouldn't have thought so, or you would be eager to marry Mike O'Donnell," she reminded me. "In your heart you feel as your mother did about 'the unsearchable riches.' 'As having nothing and yet possessing all things' means more to you than being the daughter of a rich family, doesn't it?"

"I suppose so, but I don't really know," I said honestly. "Your faith would stand up to any test, Mary; I'm not sure about mine."

"That's because you've let your aunt make you unsure of yourself," she said perceptively. "Miss Haughton can only see one way and it's a terribly narrow way. She forgets about the 'other sheep.' "

"Other sheep?" I echoed.

"Christ said, 'Other sheep I have, which are not of this fold: them also I must bring.' He didn't say that He cared less about them; just that they were different. You've been trying to shape yourself to the Haughtons' pattern and you've become discouraged because you've failed. Surely you realize now that you were never designed to be like them," she said reasonably. "You aren't the archdeacon's daughter. You're the daughter of Grace and David Amberton, born of their mutual love— and faith and courage. Isn't that a nice thought?"

"Daughter of Grace—" I repeated, my lips twisting. "That doesn't sound like me. She isn't a real person to me; I can't visualize her at all."

"I think it has a lovely sound, and it's true in a deeper sense too." Mary wasn't a demonstrative girl but she suddenly put her arm around me as we sat side by side on my bed, and gave me an affectionate squeeze. "Of course, it must seem strange to you now—two unknown parents, without even a snapshot of them—and possibly unknown relatives too in Port Petroc."

"It makes me feel as if I don't belong anywhere," I said wryly.

"I'm sure Dad will give you some time off to recover from the accident. Why don't you go down to Port Petroc?" she suggested. "You wouldn't have to make yourself known to the Trevinions, if they're still at the manor, but you could see them, and talk to people who would remember your mother. It would help you to get a clearer picture of her and why she acted as she did."

"That's a good idea. Mary, you're a lifesaver!" I responded

51

impulsively, my imagination catching fire. "That's just what I will do. I'm in such a muddle now that I can't think clearly. Perhaps if I went right away I could sort things out. There wouldn't be anyone to press me to do this or that. I don't want to leave Mother while she's ill, but—"

"It might be easier for her if you weren't here. For Dorothea too," Mary said meditatively as I hesitated.

"For Dorothea? How does she come into it?"

"Hasn't it ever occurred to you that Dorothea can't help resenting the close bond between you and your mother? She feels left out. She may be her father's daughter, but she needs your mother too. Even though she clings to your aunt, they're not as much alike as you may imagine. Dorothea is basically a shy and lonely person. She hasn't Miss Haughton's built-in self-assurance," Mary said slowly. "She came into the library yesterday evening to return your father's library books. I asked her if she had been to the hospital, and she blushed. 'Lyra wouldn't want to see me,' she said, as if I'd hit a sore spot. 'Lyra's never had much use for me.' "

"Dorothea said that?" I asked incredulously. "How absurd! It's the other way around; she has always shied away from me."

"As I see it, she's secretly yearning for affection, but too shy to meet people halfway. James said she was obviously grateful to him for taking her to the Music Club, but she was a terrible flop there. She just didn't have anything to say to any of his friends. He vowed he wouldn't ask her out again. She just didn't mix well."

I was feminine enough to be gratified by that, because I was still resentful of that invitation of James' which had been responsible for my accepting Mike's. But I wasn't spiteful enough to be glad that Dorothea had been "a terrible flop." I was frankly surprised; I had thought her abnormally self-possessed for her age. It certainly hadn't dawned on me that diffidence might make her ape Aunt Clara's manner in self-defense.

"I supposed she hadn't visited me because she took Father

52

and Aunt Clara's view of the whole terrible episode," I said in perplexity.

"I think it's more probable that she feels guilty because she went to the club with James that evening and left you up in the air," Mary told me. "Anyway, give her a chance, and a bit of encouragement. There's a lot to Dorothea, but it's all bottled up inside her. Let her feel that she matters to you. Now you'd better lie down till suppertime or your head'll be throbbing again."

5

MARY, AS USUAL, had given me food for thought. After she had gone, I stretched out on my bed and tried to sort my muddled emotions. In her sane and practical way, Mary had made me ashamed of my first resentment toward my unknown mother. It wasn't, I saw now, fair or kind to judge her until I knew more about her.

Perhaps I had always been too ready to jump to unfounded conclusions. I supposed I was prone to feel too much and not to think enough. I had taken it for granted that Dorothea shared Aunt Clara's disapproval of me. Ever since I had left school, I had seen as little of either of them as possible. Because I had imagined that Dorothea had rebuffed my friendship and affection, I had ceased to offer her either. Had I been unfair to her?

Perhaps it had been selfish of me to cling so closely to Mother as the only one of the family who really loved me. Perhaps I had tended to monopolize her and to exclude Dorothea. That simply hadn't occurred to me.

The door opened quietly. I had switched off the light, but the hall light showed Dorothea, peering round the door.

"Hello!" I said, sitting up and reaching for the switch of the bedside lamp. "Come in, stranger!"

"I didn't want to disturb you if you were asleep." She closed the door and came over to me, a faint flush staining her pale cheeks. She added jerkily, "I hope you're feeling better."

"Yes, thank you. They haven't taken the stitches out yet, but Dr. Frencham says the cut is healing nicely."

"That's good! It must have been very painful, but—you might have been killed."

I glimpsed what appeared to be genuine concern in her pale blue eyes, instead of the accusation I had expected.

"I'm surprised that I wasn't, from the reckless way Mike was driving," I said with feeling, giving her a direct, challenging glance. "Or, don't you believe that he was at the wheel."

Her color deepened, but she met my gaze steadily. "If you say so, of course I believe you," she answered unhesitatingly. "As I told Father and Aunt Clara, you would never lie to protect your own skin."

"Well, thanks," I said, ashamed of myself for having misjudged her.

She sat down on the end of my bed, tentatively and a little clumsily. All her movements were stiff or awkward. I suddenly realized how young she was. Her prim blouse and gray cardigan, her long pleated skirt, and the old-fashioned knot in which she secured her fair hair, made her look years older than her actual age.

"If it had been the other way around and you had been trying to cover up for Mike O'Donnell, it would have been different. You would do almost anything for those you love, wouldn't you?" she said almost wistfully. "Only, I didn't see how you could have fallen in love with that man. Has he really asked you to marry him?"

"Yes. Aunt Clara thinks I should jump at the chance, but I don't even like him. I certainly don't trust him, and I despise him for his attempts to clear himself of this mess," I said flatly. "Money talks; that's his pet phrase. Do you think it should talk to *me*?"

"Oh, no!" Her blue eyes widened. "Aunt Clara couldn't have meant that."

"She meant it," I said grimly. "She thought it would make

everything easier for Father if I played along with Mike, pleaded guilty, and got engaged to him."

"But you couldn't. Not if you weren't driving. You couldn't tell a lie in court," Dorothea protested, clearly horrified by the suggestion. "Mike couldn't expect you to perjure yourself for him."

"He does. He warned me that nobody would believe my denial anyway. Father obviously doesn't."

Her high forehead furrowed in a worried frown. After a pause, she said defensively, "Father's a bit hasty sometimes, and he heard Mike's version first. It did sound convincing—"

"I don't doubt it, but apparently it hasn't convinced *you*?"

"You don't think I would take the word of a man like that against yours, do you?" she said stiffly, but with an undercurrent of hurt. "I know you too well. You do crazy things sometimes, but you always own up to them. You don't care what people think of you; that's what exasperates Aunt Clara. When she finds fault with you, you just shrug your shoulders or snap back at her."

"I care all right, but I gave up trying to please Aunt Clara years ago. She has never been fair to me, but I understand why now. Did she tell you?"

"About your having been adopted?" Dorothea gave me a tentative embarrassed smile. "Yes. She told me last night. It was a relief to have it out in the open at last."

"At last? What do you mean?"

She pleated her skirt nervously in her fingers and looked away from me.

"There were always rumors at school. Perhaps you didn't hear them, but I did," she answered uncomfortably. "People used to hint that Mummie must have been married before because of your red hair and green eyes. It worried me, but I never had the nerve to ask Mummie."

"It never even entered my head. I just thought I must be a throwback," I admitted. "We ought to have been told years ago."

"Now that you know, do you mind much?"

I paused, and then answered frankly, "Not really. In a way,

56

it's a relief. It's been terribly hard sometimes, trying to measure up to the Haughton standards and realizing that I never could."

"I had no idea you felt like that, Lyra. You've always seemed so sure of yourself," Dorothea said blankly.

"*You* have," I amended.

"I? Oh, no! At school I was always being expected to 'shine' as you did, and I felt like a failure because I couldn't. I hated being compared with you," she demurred. "It was awful of me, I know, but I was jealous of my brilliant older sister. Didn't you guess?"

"Never! I envied you for being a real Haughton."

Suddenly we were both laughing half sheepishly. I felt a warm surge of affection toward Dorothea. I had misjudged her, as Mary had said.

"If only we'd been told that we weren't related, it would have been simpler for both of us," she said in a rush. "I used to have a horrible feeling that Mother had loved your father better than mine, and that was why you meant more to her."

"She never even saw my father. She was just trying to make it up to me because I didn't have any parents of my own—"

The door swung open and Aunt Clara came in, eyeing us severely.

"I don't know what you two girls are giggling about, but it's suppertime and the table isn't set yet," she pronounced. "Your father's fretting because the parish magazines haven't been mailed. I haven't had time to address them. Can you take care of them, Dorothea?"

"Yes, of course." Dorothea sprang up, still smiling, but at me, not at Aunt Clara. "We've been talking about Lyra's adoption, and wishing we'd known years ago."

"Better late than never," Aunt Clara said tritely. "Truth will come out, like bad blood."

"It doesn't make any real difference though. I mean, Lyra still belongs to us," Dorothea added. I was touched by the warmth of her tone. "We don't have to think the worst of her mother. Perhaps she was desperately hard up and couldn't afford to keep her baby."

Aunt Clara sniffed, and I said swiftly, "It wasn't that way. My father had been killed in an air raid and my mother was ill. I know about them now. Mummie has just given me the letter my own mother left for me."

"There was a letter? And your mother kept it to herself all these years?" Aunt Clara looked shocked and incredulous. "How wrong of her! She should have shown it to your father at once; he tried hard to trace your parents."

She swept aside my explanation of the sealed envelope, declaring indignantly that Mother shouldn't have promised to keep it for me, and that there had been no good reason for such secrecy. Then she added acidly that one couldn't believe anything my mother had written anyway, because a woman who would abandon her baby was plainly not to be trusted.

"You don't know anything about her," I flashed.

"Actions speak louder than words," Aunt Clara retorted, and stalked on downstairs.

I was seething, but Dorothea said pacifically: "Why do you let poor Aunt Clara upset you?"

"Poor Aunt Clara?" I echoed incredulously.

"Aren't you sorry for her? I am. She's afraid to trust anyone except Father. It's because she was terribly disappointed when she was young," Dorothea said. "I doubt if she ever told you that she was engaged to a man whom she adored and was going to go to India with him. Then, just before the wedding, her father had a stroke. Aunt Clara felt it was her duty to nurse him, but her fiancé refused to postpone his arrangements. He went off without her and met someone else in India. As you know, Grandfather was helpless for years, and Aunt Clara looked after him until he died.

"Naturally I knew about Grandfather, but not about her frustrated romance. That was tough luck, but she didn't have to let it sour her."

"I suppose it left her with a sense of insecurity. Perhaps she secretly longed for a husband and children but was afraid to let herself fall in love again. I can understand that, can't you?"

"No," I answered candidly. "Men aren't all alike. I was hurt when James dropped me as soon as he knew I wasn't Father's own daughter, but I didn't sit around and mope. I went out with Mike. I wish I hadn't, but I couldn't have guessed what would happen."

"Don't! I feel guilty about having accepted James' invitation—"

"You don't need to," I said hastily. "I've no use for a man who can't take me as I am, no matter who my parents were."

"But—you know about them now?"

I nodded. Curious to see her reaction because it had given me a shock to realize how little I had understood her, I showed her my precious documents.

Her forehead furrowed as she read my mother's letter.

"She took a terrible risk. How could she give her baby away to strangers?" she said in obvious perplexity. "If she had a family of her own, surely they would have loved you for her sake? Her illness must have clouded her mind."

"That's how I feel about it, but Mary thinks she was right."

"It turned out all right, but it might not have. And it was hard on her parents; they lost her and their grandchild. I wonder if they're still alive."

"I'm wondering too. I thought of going down to Port Petroc and making some inquiries," I said tentatively.

"Oh, yes! You should! Better late than never, as Aunt Clara would say," she agreed. "It's nice to think that your father was a clergyman; that'll be a relief to Father. Aunt Clara told me he was afraid your parents must have been traveling musicians or something to do with entertaining—the 'here today and gone tomorrow' kind, she meant. Now I must set the table. Do you feel well enough to come down to supper or shall I bring yours up on a tray?"

"That's a kind offer, but I'm just a little shaky. I would rather come down. I have to show Father these documents," I said reluctantly. "I hope he won't be angry with Mummie for having hidden that envelope."

"If he is, he won't take it out on her; he's too fond of her. He was really upset when she collapsed," Dorothea answered reassuringly.

I suppose I should have guessed that loyalty to his wife would prevent Father from commenting on her suppression of that sealed envelope.

All he said was, "It would have been a weight off our minds if Grace Trevinion—or rather Grace Amberton—had given us these certificates when she gave us her baby. We could have made inquiries and found out whether or not there were any relatives."

"She was evidently afraid that her own family would take me," I ventured.

"So it would appear," Father said drily. "That would undoubtedly have caused your mother—both your mothers—considerable grief and distress."

"It would have saved you considerable anxiety and expense, Herbert," Aunt Clara said tartly.

"Expense?" He shook his graying head. "I was fully prepared for the expense of adopting Lyra. It was a small price to pay for the blessing she was to Anne at that crucial time. Anxiety, yes, a major part of which might have been avoided had we been acquainted with her background."

"You certainly took a risk," I said, realizing fully for the first time since Aunt Clara had broken the news to me how unsatisfactory my "background" might have been, and how the numerous possibilities must have haunted a man in Father's position. I added impulsively, "I'm sorry, Father. Sorry for the occasions when I've heightened your anxiety, I mean."

"As to that, I have always believed that environment and upbringing are much more important than heredity," he answered reflectively. "In most ways, you've been a credit to us, my child. If you could learn to curb your tendency to over-emotionalism and rash impulses, you wouldn't be such an anxiety."

"It's obvious that she takes after her mother," Aunt Clara

said coldly. "It looks as if Grace Trevinion quarreled with her family and ran away from home to marry a young clergyman who should have known better than to take a wife before he had a parish and a home to offer her."

"We shouldn't make snap judgments, my dear," Father said judicially. "We have to remember that in those troubled, hazardous years, life was far from normal. Many young people married quickly and sometimes unwisely."

"If he was young, he might have volunteered for a chaplaincy in one of the services," Dorothea contributed. "Then, Grace Trevinion would naturally have been eager to marry him before he was assigned."

"Possibly, but such speculations are futile," Father reminded her. "We can, of course, make inquiries, but it seems obvious that both Lyra's parents died when she was a baby."

"There might be some Trevinions alive. I thought I might go down to Port Petroc and find out about them," I said tentatively.

To my relief, both Father and Aunt Clara approved of that suggestion. Father said kindly that a brief change would do me good, and give me a chance to think things over carefully. Aunt Clara hinted that if my maternal grandparents were still alive they might wish to recompense my foster parents for all they had done for me.

Father frowned at that. "I wouldn't even consider accepting any financial recompense from them," he pronounced. "Lyra is legally my daughter and Anne's; we made ourselves responsible for her when we adopted her. She may feel some natural inclination to contact Grace Amberton's family, but there's nothing more involved. This is Lyra's home."

That didn't sound as if he were anxious to have me off his hands. Perhaps I had misjudged him too.

"At least, it'll give all the gossip about that horrible accident a chance to die down," Aunt Clara said tartly. "It's most embarrassing to be asked just how much there is between Lyra and young O'Donnell, especially as Lyra herself refuses to give me a straight answer."

"I thought I had made it clear that there wasn't anything," I said defensively. "I barely know Mike. He's simply trying to use me to get himself out of a jam."

Father gave me a penetrating and appraising glance at that but, before he could make any comment, the front doorbell pealed.

Dorothea got up and went out to open the door. Assuming that the visitor was someone to see Father, I began to help Aunt Clara clear the table. A woman came in to do the cleaning, but Aunt Clara did most of the cooking. Dorothea and I took turns helping her, and Mother did all the mending. Mother was an expert needlewoman and knitter.

Dorothea came back, slightly flushed, to announce, "It's James Mallard. He wants to see you, Lyra. He's in the drawing room."

"Oh!" I said uncertainly.

"About your statement to the police probably." Father's grizzled brows met. "You'll have to decide what you're going to say to them. Now that you're out of the hospital, there can't be any further delay."

As I nodded and headed for the door, Dorothea said: "Lyra will have to tell what really happened, even if it does infuriate the O'Donnells."

James was standing on the rug before the fireless hearth, clasping a large box of chocolates. He thrust the box at me awkwardly and, also awkwardly, stooped to brush my forehead with his lips.

"How are you, Lyra? I've been terribly worried about you," he said. "We all have. Are you sure it was wise to leave the hospital so soon?"

"I'm practically all right again now. Sit down, James," I said hurriedly, stooping to switch on the electric heater.

Already the room, though scrupulously clean, had a chilly, unlived-in air. With Mother in bed and me in the hospital, there had been no one to use it, no one to create the flower arrangements in which we both delighted. When there were no flowers in the vicarage garden, I often drove out into the surrounding countryside for ferns and evergreens and berries.

Except when we were entertaining guests, Mother and I

were the only ones who used the drawing room. Father worked and interviewed people in his large, comfortably furnished study while Dorothea worked in her bedroom, where she had her desk and armchairs and bookcases. Aunt Clara, when she wasn't with Father, was usually in the kitchen. Her idea of relaxation was to sit in the old-fashioned rocking chair close to the stove and crochet.

If I left home, would Aunt Clara and Dorothea ever sit here with Mother during the evenings? I wondered with a pang. Had they felt excluded by the close companionship between Mother and me? Had they imagined that we didn't need or welcome anyone else? We shouldn't have let Dorothea feel that way. Why hadn't I realized it before?

James seated himself stiffly in an armchair facing mine. "You look as if you're still under the weather," he said. "Do you feel well enough to talk?"

"Yes. Only, what is there to talk about, James?"

I looked at him thoughtfully. I had known him for years, yet suddenly, familiar though I was with his every feature, his every mood and his every gesture, there was a strangeness between us. I couldn't believe that I had been almost in love with him; that I had taken it for granted that one day we would be married.

"Plenty," he said briefly, a faint color staining his fair skin. "What's the matter? Were you hurt because I didn't visit you in the hospital? I wanted to, but Father thought I'd better not. As Mother said, there was enough gossip about you already, and it was just as well not to add to it."

"You didn't want to get involved," I said. "That's what you mean, isn't it?"

"I suppose you could put it that way," he said uneasily. "You seemed to be in an awkward position. You should have had more sense than to go gallivanting around with that wild Irishman."

"Yes," I agreed calmly, though I was seething inwardly. "Just one of my misguided impulses. Do we have to discuss it? I'll make my statement to the police tomorrow, and then it'll all be up to them."

"You'll be careful, won't you? They'll ask you to sign your statement, and they'll use it," he said anxiously.

"I know; I'll say as little as possible. I don't want to make things worse for Mike, but I can't perjure myself on his behalf. I wasn't driving his car. If he had even suggested it, I would have refused."

"You must have known that his license had been suspended. If the police accept your version, they may charge you with aiding and abetting him in driving without a license or insurance," James warned me. "That's a serious offense."

"I didn't know. I had heard he had his license suspended early in the year, but I didn't realize that he hadn't gotten it back yet. As a matter of fact, I didn't even think about it. He asked me to go with him, and I accepted on the spur of the moment. You can guess why."

James shifted uncomfortably in the armchair.

"I'm sorry about that! It seemed like a good idea at the time; it was Mother's suggestion," he said jerkily.

"That's how things happen. You let your parents do your thinking for you. I was hurt, and I suppose I was curious about Mike," I said wearily. "There's no point in arguing about it now. If the police do bring any charges against me, I'll just have to answer them as well as I can."

"It's not as simple as that. It's terribly awkward for Father; the O'Donnells are valued clients of his."

"I see!" Indeed, I saw the Mallards' predicament only too clearly. I worked for them and they were personal friends of ours. Naturally Father had expected Walter Mallard to defend me, but, if I stuck to my story, he certainly couldn't represent Mike too. Would he risk antagonizing the powerful O'Donnells for friendship's sake? It would be a hard decision for him to make, and it was easy to guess what he would do. I tilted my chin. "I wouldn't want your father to lose such influential clients, James. Tell him that! I don't really need a lawyer anyway."

He stared down at his shoes in embarrassment.

"You were badly injured. If you were to plead that you had

64

blacked out and couldn't remember any details, it would be simpler for all of us," he said hesitantly.

"Yes, but it wouldn't be true. So let's drop it!" I answered impatiently.

"You're always so stubborn," he said regretfully. "You must take after your mother. After Grace Trevinion, I mean. Mary told me about her. Are you going to look up her family?"

"I thought of going down to Cornwall and finding out something about them, if your father will give me another week or so from the office."

"Of course he will. To get away for a while will be the best thing for you," he said promptly. "I could drive you down to Cornwall next weekend if you've had the stitches removed by then."

"Next weekend?" I wasn't sure that I wanted to go on such a long drive with James. Somehow the accident seemed to have snapped the old, easy comradeship between us. He might be ready to pick up the threads again now that he knew that my parents hadn't been "undesirable characters," but was I? "Thank you, James. I'll have to think about it. Next weekend will be Dorothea's midterm holiday. I haven't heard yet if she has made any plans for it."

"If she hasn't, why not take her with you? It would be a change for her, and you don't look well enough yet to be on your own," he pronounced with a mixture of exasperation and affection.

"That's a good idea," I conceded, realizing that I probably would feel stranded all alone in a strange place. "I'll see what Dorothea thinks about it."

6

MIKE'S HERE?"

I was packing my suitcase. I sat back on my heels, feeling as if I had been sharply jabbed in the ribs.

Dorothea nodded. "He insists on seeing you."

"Why?" I asked helplessly. "Why can't he leave me alone? I've made my statement; he must know that I won't retract it. What does he want?"

She gave me a thoughtful speculative glance.

"*You*—from the sound of it." She paused, then added as if reluctantly, "He's certainly very attractive. He even turned his charm on me. Don't you feel anything at all for him, Lyra?"

"What would you expect me to feel?" I countered.

"I'm wondering," she said hesitantly, "if he really cares for you."

"He has a queer way of showing it! He makes me feel like a cat treed by a large and dangerous dog. It's his own skin he's concerned about, not mine," I said bitterly. "Couldn't you get rid of him?"

"I did tell him that you were busy packing, but he said he would wait until you had ten minutes to spare. He meant it too," she assured me. "Hadn't you better see him before Father and Aunt Clara come back from that committee meeting?"

I scrambled to my feet, shaken by the prospect of another encounter between Mike and Father. Mike had lied to Father after the accident, plausibly enough to convince him. He might insist now that there was something between us, and Aunt Clara, at any rate, would believe him, even if Father didn't. Aunt Clara, I strongly suspected, was still hoping that I would silence all the gossip by announcing my engagement to Mike.

I crossed to the dressing table and ran a comb gingerly through my hair, pulling it forward to hide the horrid, jagged scar which still disfigured my forehead. I had been assured that it would fade in time, but it looked very ugly now; and I wasn't likely to forget that Mike was responsible for it.

"He's in the drawing room. I'll be in the kitchen; if you want me, just call," Dorothea said, squaring her shoulders. "I'm not afraid of him."

"Thanks, Thea," I murmured, warmed by her evident readiness to defend me. "I'm sure I can take care of him. No doubt he'll be angry with me for having given him away, and that won't be pleasant, but what else can he do?"

"He can't threaten you with anything, can he?" she asked.

"Of course not. Honestly, I don't know him much better than you do," I protested. "Aunt Clara may imagine that I've been meeting him secretly for months, but it isn't true. That night of the accident was the only time I had ever been out with him."

"Then you don't have to worry," she said in obvious relief.

I was bewildered rather than worried. I couldn't guess what Mike hoped to gain by pursuing me. No doubt the police had already confronted him with my statement. I had made it as brief and dispassionate as I could, but it was obviously a flat contradiction of his.

He was standing by the hearth when I opened the drawing room door. I had been bracing myself to face his wrath. Instead, he swung around to greet me with one of his flashing smiles, and thrust a bouquet of beautiful red carnations into my hands.

"How are you, my sweet? You're looking better," he said, gazing down at me, for all the world as though the state of my health really mattered to him. "What's all this about packing? Going away? Running out on me?"

"It's my sister's midterm break, and we're going down to Cornwall for the weekend," I answered.

"Only for the weekend?" he said, as if relieved.

"I may stay on for a few days; it depends."

"Depends on what?"

"Whether I can trace any of my mother's family or not. I've discovered that she came from Port Petroc."

"Oh? That's interesting. But don't you let any unknown relatives take possession of you. You belong here in Kelchester. You were legally adopted, weren't you?"

"Yes." I had an impulse to add, if it's any concern of yours, but that would have sounded rude.

I could smell the spicy fragrance of the carnations. I stared down at the lovely blooms, confused and embarrassed. Why had Mike brought me flowers? I wasn't in the hospital now.

"You'll have to come back for the court case, anyway," he said, as if reassuring himself.

"I know. I'm sorry about that, Mike," I said awkwardly.

"Oh, well—" He shrugged his shoulders. "I can take my medicine. If I have to, that is. I'll stick to my story, naturally. It'll depend on which one of us the judge believes."

"I suppose so."

There was a brief pause. Then he put one hand on my arm and drew me down onto the settee.

"I've been a fool. I shouldn't have expected you to cover up for me," he said abruptly. "Don't hold it against me, Lyra. It was for your sake, as well as my own and my family's, that I wanted to avoid a lot of unpleasant publicity."

I wasn't sure whether I believed that or not.

I said stiffly, "You must have known what would happen if you were caught driving while your license was suspended."

"I took a chance; one chance too many," he said ruefully. "My biggest regret is that I involved *you* in the consequences. Are you going to forgive me for it?"

68

"Yes, of course. If it matters."

"*You* matter," he said with emphasis, and every appearance of sincerity. "Can't you get it into your head that I want to marry you?"

That took me by surprise. I had been certain that his tentative proposal had been made merely to win me over and prevent me from telling the police the truth.

"You do?" I said incredulously. "Still? But why?"

"Because I'm in love with you. Why else?" he said impatiently. "Oh, I've played around with other girls, but I knew all along that you were the one I had to have! No one else will do. Can't you believe that?"

"It doesn't make sense. We're almost strangers, and we haven't anything in common," I said helplessly.

"Is there ever much sense about falling in love? Either it happens, or it doesn't. Who's to say how or why?" he demanded. "I tried hard enough to convince myself that the archdeacon's daughter wasn't in my line! But it didn't work; I couldn't stop thinking about you. Oddly enough, your exasperatingly stubborn insistence on doing what you believed to be the right thing has merely made me all the more determined to marry you."

"Mike, don't!" I said desperately. "It's no use; I couldn't ever care about you in that way."

"How do you know? Can't you forget your prejudice and give me a chance to prove that I'm not just a wild, irresponsible playboy?" he said persuasively.

I was utterly shocked. I had been bracing myself to face his anger or his reproaches, but his courtship was something I hadn't anticipated. He reached for my hand, and I felt my fingers shaking in his caressing grasp.

He was handsome, as even Dorothea had perceived. There was a kind of magnetic vitality about him. Even though he had been deplorably spoiled by his overindulgent parents, there seemed to be a basic honesty in him. Spirit and courage too. With all his failings, Mike was more of a man than James. Mike didn't care who or what my parents had been, and he would never look out for himself as James had.

"You could love me if you would let yourself," he persisted. "There isn't anyone else, is there?"

I shook my head in confusion. If I had ever cherished any dreams of marrying James, they had been roughly shattered, not by any sudden action on his part, but by his lawyerlike caution and prudence. A man who looked for references and a pedigree with his prospective bride certainly wasn't the man for me.

Moreover, from the eagerness with which Dorothea had agreed to his suggestion of driving us both down to Port Petroc, I had realized that she really liked him. Once that would have upset me, but not now. If James was Dorothea's notion of an ideal husband, she was welcome to him. It would, from every aspect, be a good match, though not exactly romantic or exciting since both of them were shy of any overwhelming, passionate emotion. I couldn't picture my young sister willingly letting herself be swept off her feet, and James had already demonstrated that his head would always rule his heart.

"Then promise to think about me while you're away," Mike said coaxingly. "Don't let your unknown relatives lure you away from Kelchester. Remember, I'll be waiting for you."

I had thought I could never trust Mike, but that evening I couldn't doubt his sincerity. I couldn't tell how deep his feeling for me went, or how long it would last, but he was evidently convinced now that he loved me.

"As my wife, you would be a somebody. You would have a lot of influence, and you would be entirely free to use it as you pleased," he added. "Doesn't that prospect have any appeal?"

"Well, of course," I said candidly.

I couldn't, in honesty, deny that I was attracted by Mike and by the material advantages he was offering me. What girl wouldn't have been? I had always felt myself something of a misfit here, but as his wife and his father's daughter-in-law I would certainly become an important person in Kelchester. Aunt Clara was well aware of that, and it was another reason why she thought I'd be foolish to turn down Mike's proposal.

It wouldn't be difficult to love Mike, I realized, but could I hope to influence him? He might promise to reform, but didn't he need a deeper incentive than his desire to please me? I wouldn't live in a house built on sand, without a sure foundation; I wanted a husband upon whom I could lean. I had a sudden conviction that, if I settled for Mike, I would be failing those unknown but obviously dedicated parents of mine.

In that poignant letter she had left for me, my mother had written of "the unsearchable riches—the only riches I want my child to value." She had added: "If you are like your father, you won't be influenced by worldly considerations."

Impulsively I freed my hands from Mike's caressive grasp.

"If you must have an answer now, it will have to be no, Mike," I said flatly.

"You don't trust me?" he said reproachfully.

"You haven't given me much reason to trust you. Actions speak louder than words," I reminded him. "And by actions I don't mean nice gestures, like bringing me these lovely flowers."

For a moment he looked disconcerted. Then his smile flashed out at me again.

"All right, my sweet! You win," he said. "I won't try to take you by storm. I'll give you all the time you need. Just promise to think of me as kindly as you can, and come back to me soon."

I went with him to the door. On the threshold, he paused. Then, swiftly, he stooped and kissed me.

"Take care of my sweetheart for me," he said—and again a tremor ran through me.

"My sweetheart?" Did he guess how alone I felt? How passionately I longed to belong to someone? To love and be loved meant infinitely more to me than anything else he had to offer. Only, I couldn't—I dare not—give my heart to a man unless I was completely sure that we could find lasting happiness together.

I knew I couldn't let Mike take advantage of the loneliness and sense of insecurity which I had been feeling ever since I had learned the facts of my adoption. That would be yielding to a more subtle form of temptation than to be swayed by the position in Kelchester he could give me.

Suddenly I realized that I was still mechanically clutching the sheaf of carnations. I decided to take them upstairs to Mother. I knew how much she loved flowers, but it would never have crossed Father's mind to buy any for her. Always practical, he would think a hothouse bouquet a sad waste of money.

Mother hadn't been downstairs yet, but she was out of bed now and seated in an armchair beside an open fire. In her faded old brown dressing gown, she looked very small and frail. Was it my imagination, or were there more gray hairs among the soft brown? A warm rush of tenderness toward her surged through me as I handed her the carnations.

"For me? Oh, darling, how lovely!" Her brown eyes lit up as she smelled the fragrant flowers. "It's been ages since I had any carnations. I remember there were some in that bouquet I was given when I opened the bazaar in aid of the children's home. Five years ago, wasn't it?"

"Yes. It must be."

"I had that new pink dress. It was so pretty but, as your aunt said at the time, not very serviceable. It showed every mark, so I had it dyed brown."

She sighed faintly, and I had a sudden wild yearning to be able to buy her all the pretty impractical things for which she secretly longed. If I were to marry Mike, I would have plenty of money. I could give Mother the small luxuries which life as a clergyman's wife had denied her. She wouldn't have to wear a faded dressing gown in dull brown or down-at-the-heel bedroom slippers if I were the wealthy mayor's daughter-in-law. She wouldn't have to feel that she had to buy things which were guaranteed to last. She could indulge her natural taste for the romantic and feminine. Perhaps, for Mother's sake, I should have listened to Mike. Or, was that another, even more subtle form of temptation?

"I've always loved carnations. We had a mass of those old-fashioned crimson ones in our Devonshire garden when you

72

were a baby," she said, smiling reminiscently. "I planted some here when we first came, but the small animals ate them."

That gave me an absurd pang. Why hadn't I paid more attention to the garden and bought the kind of plants for it which would have delighted Mother? I loved her devotedly, and yet there were so many little things I could have done for her and hadn't.

I felt bitterly ashamed of the way I had taken her for granted. Most children, I supposed, tended to accept a mother's care and devotion as their due, but I was in a different position. Mother hadn't been obliged to adopt me and treat me as her own child. I was conscious now that I owed her a debt which I could never hope to repay.

"We'll put some more carnations in this autumn," I said impulsively, and she sighed.

"If you come back from Port Petroc," she said wistfully. "The Trevinions are sure to want to keep you."

"Oh, no! They didn't approve of their daughter's marriage. They're not likely to be very interested in me," I said hurriedly. "Anyway, you'll always come first, darling. You must know that."

"I shouldn't be selfish," she said, as if trying to brace herself. "If they can do more for you than we can, and offer you a fuller life—"

Her voice trailed away and I said crisply, "My life is full enough; don't worry."

I got a vase for the carnations and arranged them for her. She watched me with a yearning expression in her eyes which made me half regret our trip to Port Petroc.

"They may be musical, and you've such a lovely voice. It's not too late for you to have it properly trained," she said suddenly. "I've felt all along that your gift was being wasted. You should be a singer not a secretary."

I hadn't thought of that. Perhaps I had inherited my voice. Had it been from Grace Trevinion? Suppose her parents were still alive, and dedicated music lovers? What if they would offer to finance my training? Would I have the fortitude to refuse? Music meant so much to me. Since Father had deliberately frustrated my ambition to be a concert singer, I had grown more or less resigned to that locked door; but how would I react if the Trevinions were eager to open it for me?

"No point in crossing bridges before we come to them," I said, giving her a reassuring smile. "Nothing and no one will ever separate me from you, Mummie. You can be sure of that."

"You're so very dear to me; you understand me," she said tremulously. "You shouldn't have bought those carnations though. They must have been expensive."

"Oh, but I didn't buy them! Mike O'Donnell brought them for us," I said hastily.

Mike had handed the flowers to me, but he hadn't said specifically that they were for me, I remembered.

"Mike O'Donnell?" A shadow crossed her expressive face. "Was he here this evening? What did he think about your visit to Cornwall?"

"He asked me not to forget him while I was away, and to come back soon."

"Then he's serious about you?"

"Yes, so it seems."

"Even though you've told the police the truth about the accident?" she asked. "Does he know that?"

"He knows. He intends to stick to his version, but he says he can take his medicine if he has to," I answered hesitantly. "He isn't a coward; I believe he has more in him than I had guessed. He really does want to marry me, and I promised to think about it while I was away."

"My darling child!" She made a little gesture of protest. "If you have to think about it, Mike obviously isn't the man for you. When you're in love, you won't have any doubts or hesitation. You'll *know*. It's a wonderful feeling; it makes the whole world seem a lovelier place. You'll feel as if your heart is singing for sheer joy, and you won't believe that you'll ever be worried or unhappy again."

"Was it like that for you?" I asked incredulously.

"It was, indeed. Life hasn't always been smooth or easy, but

I have never for one instant regretted loving your father. I'm still proud and happy to be his wife," she said firmly.

"Really and truly? Sometimes he's so impatient and intol erant," I said doubtfully. "He doesn't seem to consider you or what you would like. The parish always comes first with him."

"Naturally. I wouldn't have it otherwise," she said defensively. "His work is his life. I knew that when I married him, and I was eager to help him. I haven't done as much in the parish as I had hoped to do, because I'm such a poor speaker and organizer; but I have tried to give him a happy and comfortable home."

"You've certainly done that," I said warmly.

"Fortunately he has had Clara to help organize parish activities, and she's never nervous when she has to speak in public; but your father has always turned to me when he has been worried or discouraged." She gave me a sweet, faintly mischievous smile. "Sometimes you've resented your aunt and thought she took too much on herself, haven't you, darling? But she has lifted a weight off my shoulders and I'm deeply grateful to her."

"I would hate to have to share my husband with his sister," I said frankly, but she shook her head.

"Clara hasn't come between us. Our love for each other has never faltered. Of course, your father has his faults, as I have mine, but love teaches one perception and tolerance and the joy of giving. 'Love seeketh not her own. . . . ' You must love a man for what he is—and as he is. Don't let yourself be influenced by any other considerations."

"You're warning me not to be swayed by Mike's good looks and charm, or his father's money and position? I get the point," I said wryly.

"Or by his feeling for you," she said gently. "You're warm-hearted and affectionate. It's natural for you to long to be loved, but just to be loved isn't enough. Unless you're sure that you love him and will go on loving him through any troubles, you must not dream of marrying him."

7

ARE YOU SURE we're on the right road?" James demanded. "We seem to be wandering aimlessly through a network of lanes."

Dorothea was seated in the back of the car, a map spread out on her lap. She was peering at it anxiously.

"We should be coming to a crossroads any minute now, and Port Petroc is straight ahead," she answered.

"Straight? There's nothing straight about these lanes," James said edgily.

We had had a pleasant, uneventful drive down from Kelchester, until we had come off the main road at Truro. Since then we had been following a series of lanes, with high banks on either side. James was a good, safe driver, but he wasn't used to country lanes. Twice he had been forced to back up close to the hedge to let a tractor and trailer pass, and he had been unreasonably vexed because trailing brambles had whipped against the car. Admittedly, it was a nice car, only a year old and in immaculate condition, but he was absurdly possessive over it. He had refused to let me help him drive, and I wondered if he still believed that I had wrecked Mike's sports car, or if he just distrusted all feminine drivers. He had, I was realizing, a patronizing air toward women which was

76

vaguely irritating. He evidently mistrusted Dorothea's map reading, even though she was extremely competent at that kind of thing. She wasn't likely to give him the wrong directions.

"It looks to me as if we've been going around in circles," James complained, and Dorothea's fair skin flushed at his tone. "We ought to get accommodations before dark."

"It can't be much farther now," she said pacifically. "It's early yet; it won't be dark for another hour at least."

"There's a sign ahead," I said hopefully. "Yes, you're right, Thea. It does say Port Petroc. Cheer up, James!"

"I think we've come by a very roundabout way," he grunted.

"From the map, it's in rather an isolated position with the sea on one side of it and a creek on the other," Dorothea reminded us.

James gave another grunt. The road from the crossroads led down a steep hill and then as steeply uphill. He shifted into lower gear with a sour expression on his face. I thought suddenly that Mike O'Donnell would have treated this last stage of our journey as an adventure and would have joked about the narrow, twisting route. He wouldn't have embarrassed us by making us feel that we were responsible for it and would be held responsible for any damage to his cherished car. James was behaving like a fussy, nervous old maid, and I nearly told him so.

Then we crawled up to the crest of the hill, and I forgot my irritation as I gazed down at the azure blue sea, the dark rocks, and the silver sand of a small cove set between towering cliffs. There were cottages and what appeared to be an inn on the cliffs, but the main part of the village lay in a wooded hollow. I saw a church tower rising from the trees, and the cool gleam of water.

"What a forsaken spot!" James exclaimed as we began to descend another winding hill.

"It's lovely," I said impulsively. "I can't imagine how Grace Trevinion could have left it for London."

"Rather lonely," Dorothea said, leaning forward to gaze

over my shoulder. "I suppose people come here in the summer, but it could be dreary in the winter."

"It's almost an island," James said as we reached the foot of the hill and crossed the narrow stone bridge over the creek. "We should have stayed overnight in Truro. I doubt if we'll find good accommodations here."

Beyond the bridge, trees rose up on either side of the narrow lane. It was almost like driving through a tunnel. We emerged from it beside the cove. To the left of us, the lane ended in a kind of bridle path among the trees. To the right, it rose steeply again to the inn and cottages on the cliff. James braked and switched off the engine.

"Well?" he demanded. "Where do we go from here? We seem to have reached the end of nowhere."

There were boats in the cove, some moored to a primitive jetty and others drawn up on the sand, but the shore was deserted except for a few sea gulls pecking among the seaweed at high-water mark. I opened the car door and sprang out, sniffing the salty tang of the clean, fresh air.

On the landward side of the lane were several cottages, a small post office, village stores, the church, and a wrought-iron gate which, I surmised, led to the vicarage. None of the cottages, as far as I could see, were displaying welcoming "Bed & Breakfast" signs. This was October, of course, and evidently the holiday season was over as far as Port Petroc was concerned.

James got out stiffly and turned to open the rear car door for Dorothea.

"Well?" he asked again in a disgruntled fashion. "What do you propose to do now, Lyra? Drive all the way back to Truro? I can't say I look forward to negotiating those lanes again, but we can hardly camp out on the beach."

"We could try the inn—if it is an inn," Dorothea said tentatively, gazing up at the house on the cliff top.

"Just a village pub from the look of it," James said disparagingly. "Hardly suitable quarters for you girls, even if it has any rooms available."

"There must be someone in the village who takes paying

guests," I said, impatient of his defeatist attitude. "We can ask."

"Where? There's no sign of life anywhere. Even the post office is closed," he said irritably.

"The vicar would know," I said hopefully.

"And where do we locate the vicar?" he demanded.

"That must be the gate of the vicarage—that gate in the shrubbery, next to the church. Shall we go and see if the vicar's at home?" I suggested.

"You can, if you like. I'd feel like a fool, landing in this dead spot and demanding accommodations at a moment's notice," James said sourly. "Why couldn't you have made inquiries before we set off on this wild-goose chase?"

"There wasn't much time, and I didn't realize that it was such a small village," I retorted. "It was your suggestion that you should drive us down here, James. You didn't have to come with us."

"It's been a long drive; poor James is tired," Dorothea interposed hurriedly. "There's no need to snap at him."

"Snap at him? I like that!" I flashed. "Does he have to keep on griping and grumbling? Anyone would think we were stranded in the desert."

"Let's not argue about it," she said uncomfortably. "Shall I come to the vicarage with you?"

"No, you'd better stay with 'poor James' and soothe his ruffled feathers," I said tartly.

It was absurd to be rattled by James' criticism of the village, I told myself, but something about the quiet, untouched beauty of this place seemed to have caught at my heartstrings. I had never been here in my life before, yet I had the strangest feeling of possessiveness toward it. A gentle breeze off the sea was stirring my hair like a caress as I walked up the lane to that iron gate. The soft splash of the waves in the cove, the cries of the sea gulls and the twittering of birds in the fine old trees were like familiar music in my ears. It was as though some part of me had come home to this remote village and recognized it.

Here in this secluded cove Grace Trevinion must have

played as a child, I thought, with a curious quickening of my pulses. She must have worshiped in that old weatherbeaten gray stone church. Her feet must have known every inch of this narrow lane. Her hands must have lifted the latch on this old-fashioned wrought-iron gate. She must have walked up this mossy, graveled drive between these high clumps of rhododendrons.

Ever since I had read her letter, my unknown mother had been a vague, shadowy, inexplicable figure to me. Now it was as if she were gradually taking a shape and substance. She had been born and bred in this lonely village. Presumably, all her early life had been spent here until she had fled away to marry my father. Had she ever thought of it longingly—been homesick for it? I wondered. Surely she must have missed the peace and the beauty. Yet she hadn't come back here. She had preferred to be evacuated to unfamiliar surroundings in Devon, among strangers, to wait for her baby's birth. According to my birth certificate, I had been born in a Plymouth hospital—

The whirr of a lawn mower brought me back to the present with a start. I stepped clear of the shrubbery and saw a wide expanse of lawn stretching from one side of the drive up to a long, low, gray-walled house. A young man in blue jeans and a thickly knit fisherman's jersey was propelling a lawn mower over the grass. As he approached, I saw that he had thick and untidy tawny brown hair and a warmly tanned skin. A fisherman turned gardener, I surmised. He pulled up on the edge of the grass beside me and glanced at me inquiringly.

"Good evening," he said, and his voice didn't sound like a fisherman's. "Were you looking for me?"

I shook my head. *He must be the vicar's son,* I thought confusedly.

"I just wanted a word with the vicar," I explained hurriedly. "Is he at home?"

"Here!" His lean, bronzed face lit up with a delightful smile. "I'm the vicar. May I help you, Miss?"

"Haughton," I said mechanically. "Lyra Haughton. I'm sorry. I didn't guess—"

I gazed up at him, confused and apologetic, and the oddest sensation gripped me. He wasn't particularly good-looking. His features were rugged—high cheekbones, a large nose, a firm mouth and an uncompromisingly square chin—but that smile illuminated them like sunshine on rock. Just as I had seemed to recognize the cove and the village, so now I seemed to recognize him. I had certainly never seen him before and I didn't even know his name, yet it was as though he was dear and familiar. I caught my breath sharply. The extraordinary part of it was that he was looking down at me as if he knew me too.

For a long moment neither of us spoke. We just stood there, looking at each other.

Then he passed one hand across his forehead, brushing the unruly brown hair back, and asked: "What can I do for you, Miss Haughton? Did you want to see inside the church?"

"I would like to sometime, very much. Only now I'm looking for somewhere to stay. For tonight and the weekend," I said in a rush. "My sister's with me, and the friend who drove us down here. We thought you might know of someone who takes paying guests."

"For how long would it be?"

"For the weekend, and perhaps till the end of next week. At least, my sister has to go home on Monday evening, but I might be staying on for a while—"

I was barely conscious of what I was saying. There was a curious trembling at my knees, and a mist in front of my eyes. I dug my nails into the palms of my hands to steady myself, but the smooth, freshly mown grass seemed to be rising in a wavering swathe of green as if to engulf me—

Then there was a firm grip on my arm, and that voice, which sounded in my ears like the echo of once loved music, was saying, "You're very pale. Have you had a long drive? I think you had better come into the house."

"Thank you," I said faintly. "It has been a long way, and I'm not quite fit again."

"You've been ill?" he asked, as if genuinely concerned.

"I was in a car accident—"

81

The scar on my forehead was throbbing painfully; in fact, I seemed to be throbbing all over. Perhaps it had been too soon to take such a long drive. Even though James was a careful driver, it had been something of a strain.

"My aunt will make some tea to revive you," he said kindly. "And she'll probably think of someone who has rooms to let. She knows most of our parishioners already."

"Your aunt does? Don't you?" I asked confusedly.

"I haven't been here for a month yet, but Aunt Araminta knows the village well. She has often stayed here; she's an artist," he explained, propelling me firmly across the grass toward the house.

There were wide stone steps leading up from the lawn to a glass door. I stumbled on the steps, but his hand on my arm steadied me. I remember the delicious scent of the new mown grass and the feel of the worn, uneven stone beneath my flagging feet. I remember the sense of comfort I experienced as those strong fingers gripped my arm, guiding me. His voice and his touch, and the kindly concerned expression in his amber brown eyes registered on me, but everything else was disconcertingly hazy.

I must have been perilously close to fainting. If he hadn't kept hold of me, I'm sure I would have collapsed on the ground. It was as though I were fumbling my way feebly through a thickening fog.

Then I heard the familiar creak of a wicker chair as he eased me into it, and he was saying authoritatively, "Just put your head down. I'll call my aunt."

I wanted to cry out, "Don't let go of me! Don't leave me!" but I bit back that childish appeal and gripped the arms of the wicker chair.

After a moment or two, that terrible feeling of faintness passed. I blinked and raised my head. I was in an old-fashioned kitchen with a stone floor and white walls. A fire was crackling cheerfully in a big black range and a teakettle was singing on top of it. There were pots of gaily colored geraniums on the wide windowsill, and a bowl of Michaelmas

82

daisies on the bare oak table. It was such a homey, peaceful setting that I felt the tension seeping out of me.

Footsteps sounded on the flagged stone of the passage, and a small, plump, gray-haired woman came in, followed by the vicar.

"Miss Haughton, my aunt, Miss Araminta Denver," he introduced us. "Miss Haughton and her sister are looking for rooms in the village for the weekend."

"No need to look any further," Miss Denver said briefly, beaming at me. "You can stay here. We've plenty of rooms. Half of them haven't been opened up yet, but there's one guest room ready. We had to put up a visiting preacher and his wife last weekend. You and your sister are more than welcome to it."

"That's very kind of you," I said hesitantly. "Only, really, we shouldn't trouble you. We thought there would be 'Bed and Breakfast' places here. We didn't realize that it was quite such a small village."

"Most of the cottagers take in guests during the summer, but not after September. No point in your traipsing around searching for a room when we've one here," she said practically. "You've come from a distance?"

"From Kelchester."

"You're looking worn out, you poor child. Just relax while I make a pot of tea," she said kindly.

"From Kelchester?" her nephew echoed, his thick brown brows meeting. "You're a stranger here? Odd—"

"Why is it odd?" I asked.

"Because I've a feeling that I've seen you somewhere. Have we met before?"

"No, and I've never been here before."

"I thought I couldn't have forgotten you if we had met, yet I have that strong sense of having known you," he said perplexedly.

My pulses gave a little leap. Had he recognized a likeness between me and members of my mother's family? Then, there must still be Trevinions here, and our trip wasn't a wild-goose chase after all.

Later I would ask him, but I felt too exhausted now to explain my mission and the few facts in my possession.

I said impulsively, "I would have remembered you if we had ever met. As it is, I don't even know your name."

"Sorry! It's Denver. Adam Denver."

Adam? I had never known an Adam before, but the name suited him, I thought, glancing up at him appraisingly. It meant "man," didn't it? And he was certainly a manly looking man, with his strong, rugged features, broad shoulders and well-built figure. He wasn't as tall as Mike, and he didn't have Mike's striking good looks, but he would never be overlooked in a crowd. I liked the way he held himself, the direct gaze of his amber brown eyes, and the hint of humor in the curve of his firmly cut lips.

He was young, but not as young as I had supposed when I had first caught sight of him pushing the lawn mower. Just on the right side of thirty, I surmised now. This was probably his first parish. I wondered why he had chosen to come to such an isolated village. Surely this was a more fitting setting for an elderly clergyman. Adam Denver looked as if he had enough strength and energy and determination to tackle a much more arduous job.

"Now then—" Miss Araminta Denver had made tea and was stirring the contents of the large brown earthenware teapot vigorously. "This'll bring some color back to your cheeks, my dear. You look as if you've been badly carsick."

"I haven't, but I was in a car accident recently. This was the first long drive I'd taken since then," I explained. "And when we arrived, the friend who drove us down here was annoyed that we hadn't stayed overnight in Truro. The village seemed so small and deserted—"

"It's always quiet at this time of day because everyone's indoors having high tea," Miss Araminta told me, "except for those fishermen who are still out in their boats. There's more of Port Petroc than you can see from the cove. There are cottages on the cliffs, and in the valley beyond. Some quite sizable houses, too, hidden by the trees, or on the other side of the creek."

84

I longed to ask where the manor was and if there were still Trevinions there but, as I sipped the hot, sweet tea gratefully, I remembered that Dorothea and James were waiting by the car. They probably were becoming impatient and wondering what I was doing. Dorothea would understand when I explained about suddenly feeling faint, but James wouldn't. He was the kind of man who shrank from any feminine weakness and had a horror of illness; that was probably an additional reason why he hadn't visited me while I had been in the hospital.

"Feeling better now?" Adam Denver asked solicitiously as he took my empty cup from me.

"Much better, thank you! I'm sorry I became faint like that, but we didn't stop for tea," I said apologetically. "I'll go and get my sister. That is, if you're really sure we won't be too much trouble, Miss Denver?"

"You'll be very welcome, child. You stay where you are and have another cup of tea. Adam will get your sister and your luggage," Miss Araminta said crisply. "We've only the one guest room ready, but your friend will be able to get a room at the Anglers' Rest on the cliffs. It's quite comfortable and never full at this time of the year."

Dorothea and I could have found accommodations there too, I supposed, but Miss Araminta might be hurt if we refused her hospitality. She seemed genuinely eager to have us, and I was certainly eager to stay.

"Right! Where shall I find your sister?" Adam inquired.

"Just down the lane. The car's parked on the shoulder, above the cove. Shouldn't I come with you?" I said hesitantly.

"No need. I can introduce myself."

Again he gave me that warm, illuminating smile. Then he turned and strode out by the glass door. He moved with the ease of an athlete. I watched him through the glass as he crossed the lawn and had to check an absurd impulse to spring up and run after him.

"Now then—" Miss Araminta said in her brisk fashion. "Explain yourself, child!"

85

"What?" I started and then realized that she was holding my refilled cup out to me. "Oh, thank you!"

There was a twinkle in her eyes—amber brown eyes like her nephew's, but narrower than his—as if she had read my thoughts, but her tone was purposeful as she demanded, "Who are you?"

That struck me as an odd question. It jerked me out of my abstraction. I stopped mentally following Adam as he strode through the shrubbery and up the lane, stopped wondering what James and Dorothea would make of him and how they would react to his aunt's invitation.

"Who am I?" I echoed in bewilderment. "My name's Lyra Haughton. My father is Archdeacon Haughton of Kelchester."

"Is that so?" She put her head on one side, considering me. "Then, what's your connection with the Trevinions?"

"With the Trevinions?" I repeated faintly. "What makes you imagine that I have any connection with them?"

"My dear child, I'm an artist, and artists have to be observant. Adam couldn't guess why he seemed to recognize you, but I saw the likeness instantly. You must be related to one of the red-haired Trevinions. To the missing daughter, perhaps, who vanished without trace during the war," she said with a hint of impatience. "There's a striking portrait of her hanging in the picture gallery at the manor."

"Is there?" I felt a tremor run through me, a tremor of excitement curiously tinged with apprehension. "There are still Trevinions at the manor?"

"Very much so. 'Black Trevinions,' as the local inhabitants call them. No more redheads. The one who ran away was the last—to the general regret."

"Why?" I asked confusedly, feeling as if she were going too fast for me. "I mean, what difference does the color of their hair make?"

"Considerable, according to local legends," she assured me drily. "The Trevinions are a very old family and apparently they've always exercised a good deal of power here. They own most of the farms and many of the cottages. Even this parish used to be in their hands, and at one time they ran the small pilchard fishing fleet. The fishing has fallen into decline but the Trevinions have retained their grip on the land. Some of them, no doubt, have been conscientious landlords. Others, in the distant past, were reputedly wreckers and smugglers. 'Black hair, black heart' is what the old people here say of them. In the past, I've been told, there were general rejoicings when a red-haired heir was born."

"Oh!" I said uneasily. "Legends? Surely people don't take old legends seriously nowadays?"

"In self-contained, somewhat isolated communities like this one, legends linger," she answered wryly. "Particularly if they appear to be based on facts. Few of our parishioners have any reason to love the Trevinions."

"You sound as if you don't like the Trevinions, Miss Denver."

She shrugged her plump shoulders.

"I scarcely know them. I certainly don't like some of the things I've heard about them."

"Village gossip?" I hazarded.

"Possibly, but no smoke without fire," she reminded me. "Rumor has it that the Trevinions drove the last vicar's wife to a nervous breakdown. I don't know whether that's true or not, but the vicar did resign from this parish after less than two years here. His predecessor stuck it out for nearly five years. He was a middle-aged widower, neither sensitive nor imaginative. When he arrived, he was a stout, happy-looking man. When he left, he was a shadow of his former self and convinced that this house was haunted. The parish was empty for nine months before Adam was persuaded to accept it."

I stared at her in perplexity. She sounded entirely calm and matter-of-fact. She didn't give me the impression that she was the kind of woman to be influenced by legends or gossip or local prejudices; she looked thoroughly normal and sensible.

"Are you implying that the Trevinions deliberately try to get rid of every vicar who comes here?" I demanded incredulously.

"Of every vicar—and everybody else—who attempts to stand up to them," she amended. "I've seen it. For many years

I've spent most of my summer holidays in Port Petroc or in the vicinity. My mother was a Cornish girl, and as a child, I used to stay with her parents who farmed on the coast near Falmouth. This part of the world will always be home to me. I had been watching events in this parish from the sidelines and becoming increasingly concerned about them, but helpless to intervene. Then—"

She paused, her forehead furrowing. Her amber brown eyes seemed to be probing and appraising me. I gazed back at her inquiringly. "Until the end of July, I was an art instructor at a girls' school in Eastbourne. Then I reached retirement age and decided to join forces with Adam. He was working as a clergyman in a large parish in London. I heard that this parish was vacant again, so I persuaded him to apply for it. Perhaps it was a mistake to involve him, but he's young and tough. I thought he would be a match for those people," she said, and paused again.

"The Trevinions?" I prompted her. "Well?"

"Exactly who are you? And what are you doing here?" she asked challengingly. "Why did you come to this house looking for Adam? Did they send you?"

"The Trevinions? No, of course not. I don't know them—any of them. It wasn't that way at all," I protested. "I wasn't looking for Adam, as you put it. I just hoped the vicar could tell us where to find rooms."

I wished she wouldn't look at me like that, as if she doubted my story and suspected me of some ulterior motive in calling at the vicarage. She had greeted me so kindly and hospitably. Now she appeared to be regretting her welcome. Why? Just because she had recognized a family likeness between me and the Trevinions. She seemed to have an obsession about the Trevinions, I reflected uneasily. Half of what she had told me didn't make sense, but she was obviously convinced of the truth of it.

"We don't have to stay here," I added stiffly. "It was your suggestion, Miss Denver. If you would prefer us to find accommodations in the village—"

"It's too late now," she cut me short. "It was too late from the moment he saw you."

"I don't understand—"

"And there's a lot I don't understand either." Again she interrupted me impatiently. "Why didn't you go to the manor?"

"Because I don't know the Trevinions, and I wasn't even sure if any of them were still living here. They're certainly not aware of my existence. I was adopted by my parents—by Archdeacon Haughton and his wife—when I was a tiny baby. I have only just discovered who my real parents were," I retorted. "As you surmised, my mother was Grace Trevinion—"

As briefly and concisely as I could, I gave her the facts of my birth and adoption.

"So, it was simply curiosity which brought you here?" she said in relief. "I thought I couldn't be that far wrong. I pride myself on being a good judge of character, and my first impulse was to welcome you. Then, when I recognized your likeness to the red-haired Trevinions and saw the way you and Adam were looking at each other, I was afraid you might bring trouble—"

I felt myself flushing hotly, but she went on as if she hadn't noticed my confusion, "That's what living here, as opposed to merely visiting the place, does to one. This atmosphere of suspicion and mistrust is terribly infectious. One can't get away from the Trevinions and their pernicious influence."

"Is it pernicious?"

"I'm very much afraid so. I can only hope that you won't be engulfed by it."

"My mother wasn't. She ran away," I reminded her.

"And you've inherited her red hair. Perhaps you'll remain immune," she said, and again her glance challenged me. "For Adam's sake—"

She checked herself abruptly. For a moment there was an embarrassing but oddly significant silence between us. Then the twinkle came back to her eyes.

"Don't mind me, child! I'm like a hen with one chick in

89

regard to that boy. His mother died when he was only seven years old, and he has always been very dear to me. I don't want him to be hurt, and I feel responsible for bringing him here. But I have to remember that he's a man now. I shouldn't act like a fussy old maid, should I?"

Again I had the sensation of being rushed along too swiftly, of being whirled through a fog, conscious of danger ahead but unable to distinguish just where it lurked. I wanted to say something to reassure her, to remind her that Adam and I were strangers, and that there was no reason at all why I should make any impact on his life. But somehow I knew that wouldn't be true. The impact had already been made—on both of us. Adam might be able to shrug it off, but I was still shaken by it.

8

THERE WAS MUCH MORE that I yearned to ask Miss Araminta. But before I could frame my questions, I saw James' car, coming slowly up the mossy drive. In a way, that was a relief. I suspected that I was in a strange overstrung, imaginative state, a prey to emotions and fantasies which I had never known before. James and Dorothea would jerk me back to normal.

"Here comes my sister," I said hurriedly. "And James."

"James?" Miss Araminta raised her eyebrows inquiringly.

"James Mallard. His father is our family lawyer. I work in their office in Kelchester," I explained. "When Dorothea and I were arranging this trip, James said he would drive us down here. His sister and I were in school together; she's my closest friend."

There was no need to mention Mary, yet I had felt compelled to add that. I didn't want Miss Araminta to imagine that James meant anything special to me. From her half smile, I realized that she had understood me, and again I was conscious that I was blushing. I really was absurdly keyed up and overemotional. Did it matter what Adam's aunt thought? Why should I be so anxious that she shouldn't reach any erroneous conclusions about me?

I sprang up, relieved to find that there was no longer any

unnerving weakness in my limbs or any hint of that disturbing dizziness. I caught a fleeting glimpse of my reflection in a small mirror on the wall. I was paler than usual, but my eyes were clear and bright, shining like emeralds.

"I expect your sister would like a cup of tea. I'll get the teapot," Miss Araminta said practically, rising and crossing to the stove. "Go get her, my dear. Adam will bring the luggage in by the front door. The front of this house is at what I call the back, facing toward the creek. That door will take you into the passage which leads to the hall."

I went out by the door she was indicating and found myself in a narrow, dimly lit, twisting passage. A number of doors opened off it. This was certainly a large house—much too large to be practicable as a present-day vicarage. After blundering into several obviously unused rooms, I eventually reached the hall. Adam was carrying our suitcases toward a wide staircase with handsome, carved oak bannisters. Dorothea was hovering uncertainly just inside the massive oak front doors. She was looking unusually flustered.

"Oh, there you are, Lyra," she hailed me with a mixture of relief and reproach. "We couldn't imagine what had become of you. Are you all right? Mr.—er—Denver said you'd had a dizzy spell."

"Yes, I suddenly felt terribly faint. I'm sorry—"

"As long as you're better now—" She eyed me anxiously. "I thought it was a mistake not to stop for tea, but James—"

She broke off as James himself came up the steps behind her, carrying our mackintoshes and Dorothea's camera. She quickly moved aside and he put them on a carved oak chest.

"That's all," he announced. "I may as well push off now and try my luck at the inn."

"Are you sure we ought to stay here, Lyra?" Dorothea asked in a lowered tone, glancing nervously toward the staircase up which Adam had vanished. "It seems odd to push ourselves on complete strangers, but he—Mr. Denver—was most insistent."

"It's the best plan," James said decisively before I could answer. "Cheaper than staying at the inn and a more suitable place for you girls, especially if Lyra's still feeling under the weather."

I flinched inwardly. It was characteristic of James to urge us to save money if we could, and equally characteristic of him to be eager to push me into someone else's hands if I were in poor health.

"I'm all right now," I said hastily.

"Then, can't we go to the inn with James? I don't want to stay here," Dorothea said urgently.

"Why not? Miss Denver wouldn't have suggested it if she had thought we would be a nuisance," I tried to reassure her.

"Of course not. Don't fuss, Thea!" James said impatiently. "I'm sure you'll be more at home here than in a fisherman's inn. I'll see you both in the morning."

He went briskly back to his car. Dorothea made as if to follow him, but he drove off without a backward glance.

"I think it's very selfish of him to leave us stranded here," she said in a tone which made me blink. I had never heard her criticize James before. "We don't know these Denvers and— and I don't like the idea of staying in this dreary old house."

I remembered that she always tended to be shy of strangers and ill at ease with them.

"They're very nice," I said, and thought what an inadequate adjective that was to describe the impression that the aunt and her nephew had made on me. "Very friendly and hospitable."

"We don't know them," she repeated stubbornly. "Is he really the vicar? He doesn't look like any parson I've ever seen."

"He was mowing the lawn when I interrupted him. You wouldn't expect him to do that in a clerical collar and a dark suit," I said soothingly. "You're tired, dear. Come and have a cup of tea and meet Miss Araminta Denver. Then you'll feel better."

I put my hand on her arm and piloted her into the passage. She shivered suddenly and clutched at my hand.

"I don't like this place. There's something weird about it. I wish we'd stayed in Truro."

93

"Well, we didn't, so it's no use wishing. Weird?" I echoed, perplexed because it wasn't like Dorothea to be nervous or fearful. "Do you mean this house or the village?"

"Both. The village is unnaturally quiet, and so isolated and remote. As for this house—" She shivered again and glanced uneasily over her shoulder. "It looks terribly old and—and as if it were haunted."

"What you need is a nice hot cup of tea," I said, in older-sister fashion. "Of course, it seems quiet here after the bustle and traffic of Kelchester."

"It's weird," she repeated. "As if it were under a spell or something. We didn't see a single person while we were waiting for you. I began to feel as if we were cut off from civilization—as if anything might happen."

That disturbed me, simply because Dorothea was normally so practical and sensible—the last person to imagine things. Yet she was perceptive, I had to admit. She had guessed years ago, in our school days, that I wasn't her father's daughter. Had she picked up vibrations of some kind as she had waited for me—vibrations of past unhappiness or deeds of violence? Somehow I couldn't scoff at her misgivings or attribute them —as I had attributed my own dizziness—to overfatigue. Dorothea was tough physically, and a long drive wouldn't exhaust her to that extent.

I gave her arm an affectionate squeeze, and ushered her into the kitchen. In the evening sunshine, still filtering through the kitchen windows, I saw that her fair skin was paler than usual, and she had a tense, apprehensive air about her. She brightened visibly as I introduced her to Miss Araminta. If Adam didn't look like a vicar, neither did his aunt look like the traditional "eccentric artist." She was so comfortably plump and homey in her russet brown blouse and skirt and a flowered apron. She poured tea for Dorothea and said cheerfully that she was very glad to have us here. This was such a large house for only two people. Next summer, she would have to think about renting out some of the bedrooms. There was always a demand for accommodations in Port Petroc

94

during the season, from people who wanted to go fishing or sailing.

Dorothea responded politely but a little awkwardly. I found it difficult to drag my eyes away from the glass door. Adam was evidently determined to finish cutting the grass before dark. I could hear the whirr of the lawn mower, and every now and then I caught glimpses of his strong, well-built figure as he propelled the machine in long, even swathes.

"Now, I'm sure you'd like to freshen up and unpack before supper," Miss Araminta observed, when Dorothea had refused a second cup of tea. "We haven't any electricity here—just oil lamps and candles. I'll put some sheets on your beds."

She led us back along that dim passage and up the wide stairs to a vast bedroom overlooking the trees to the creek. It was nicely but rather sparsely furnished. Miss Araminta got the sheets and we helped her to make up the two beds. Then, having lit the oil lamp on the dressing table and shown us the old-fashioned bathroom across the passage, she left us to do our unpacking.

I opened the casement window and leaned out, gazing through the failing light across the creek. On the far side, which was heavily wooded, I could see chimneys rising above the trees. To judge from the number and extent of the chimneys, a large house stood among the trees. Could it be the manor? I had an irrational conviction that it was.

As I watched, two dark figures emerged from a barely visible path through the trees and approached a boat which was drawn up above the creek. From this distance, they looked so absurdly identical in height and dress—windbreakers and jeans—that they might have been twins. My long-distance sight was exceptionally good. Even in the dusk, I could distinguish them and their movements quite clearly. They were loading lobster pots from a pile on the bank into the boat.

"What is it? What are you looking at, Lyra?" Dorothea asked behind me.

"Those two with the boat."

"Where?" She came to lean beside me. "I can't see anyone."

"Over on the other side of the creek."

"I can only just make out the gleam of water," she said regretfully.

"Listen! They've pushed the boat down to the water and they're starting the engine. I suppose the creek leads into the sea somewhere. There must be another cove. They wouldn't be laying lobster pots in the cove, would they?"

"I've no idea. Does it matter?" she said in bewilderment. "Why are you interested?"

"Because they came from the big house among the trees. It could be the manor, and they could be Trevinions."

"Oh? Have you asked the Denvers about the Trevinions?"

"Yes. At least, Miss Araminta spoke about them. She recognized a family likeness between me and a portrait of Grace Trevinion which she had seen at the manor."

Dorothea was silent for a moment. Then she said in a stiff, restrained tone, "You must be pleased that you've located the family so quickly. Are your mother's parents alive?"

"I don't know. Miss Araminta didn't mention them."

"The vicar must know."

"Yes, but—" I was conscious of muddled and conflicting emotions. I turned to her impulsively. "I'm not going to ask him. Please don't tell him why we're here."

"Why in the world not?" she demanded blankly.

"Because I'm not sure that I want to contact the Trevinions."

"You don't? But that was the whole object of our trip," she reminded me in frank astonishment.

"To find out about them. Not necessarily to claim kinship with them," I amended. "From what Miss Araminta said, there's some strange kind of hostility between the manor and the vicarage."

"Hostility? You mean that the Trevinions don't approve of this vicar? Perhaps they're old-fashioned, or as rigid as Aunt Clara."

"Oh, no! It isn't a question of objecting to him personally— to his casual dress or his outlook. It's much more involved because they were against both his predecessors too. I haven't

96

figured out why as yet," I tried to explain. "They may just be antichurch."

"That's strange," she said uneasily. "Usually a squire supports the church and vicar."

"Exactly. I must find out more about the situation before I make any move toward the Trevinions—if I ever do."

"*If?* You were so anxious to get acquainted with them."

There was a hint of resentment in her tone, which I couldn't ignore.

"Out of curiosity," I said hurriedly. "Not because I had any idea of hitching myself on to them. Mummie's my mother and you're my sister. I couldn't feel the same way about Grace Trevinion's family."

"I'm glad of that," she said, her tone softening. "It would be a terrible blow to Mother if you deserted us. To Father too. In his own undemonstrative fashion, he is fond and proud of you."

"He hasn't had much reason to be either, but I am truly grateful to him for—for everything," I said. "Don't ever think I'm not. That's why I don't want to become involved with the Trevinions if they're not his—our—kind of people."

It was one reason, at any rate, I amended mentally. The other, which I was scarcely ready to admit even to myself, concerned Adam. If the Trevinions were against him, then I was against them; it was as simple as that.

"It's getting chilly. Better close that window," Dorothea said abruptly.

As I turned to comply, I heard the chug-chug of a motor-boat. It sounded like a powerful motor, and already the boat was almost out of sight. Lightless, like a dark streak on the water, it was vanishing under that old narrow bridge.

I closed the window and Dorothea put her hand over mine in an awkwardly affectionate gesture.

"Lyra, don't be upset if the Trevinions aren't all you would like them to be. I've been thinking about that letter you showed me," she said jerkily. "Grace—your mother—said it wasn't a Christian home, didn't she? Perhaps they've always had some grudge against the church."

97

"Perhaps," I agreed. "Anyway, let's watch our steps and not say too much. I don't have to make myself known to them."

She nodded, looking relieved. I was touched that she was obviously reluctant to surrender me to my unknown relatives.

We unpacked what we would need for the night. Then, hand in hand like children, we fumbled our way down the wide staircase.

"We should have brought flashlights," Dorothea said as she bumped into the oak chest when we crossed the dark hall. "James has one in his car; we'd better borrow it tomorrow. I never guessed that there wouldn't be any electricity here."

"The farms must have it. Perhaps the line goes to the cliffs but not down this way. This part of the village is in a dead end."

"It certainly seems like one."

Appetizing aromas reached our nostrils as we groped our way down the passage. The kitchen was quite brightly lighted by two oil lamps. The table was laid for four, but Miss Araminta was alone.

"Adam was called out to old Mrs. Williams'. She has been recovering from a stroke, but evidently she just had another. She's nearly ninety, so her chances of survival aren't too good," she said regretfully. "It's a pity because she has been one of the staunchest members of our small congregation, and she has kept her family in line."

"I suppose it's a very small parish?" Dorothea inquired.

"It covers quite an area—Port Petroc and two villages—Trevinion and Mawnan St. Kevin—but the population is small and growing steadily smaller," Miss Araminta answered. "Very few young married couples stay. Either they don't care for being employed by the Trevinions, or else they can't find anywhere to live. The Trevinions stubbornly oppose any building projects."

"Can they?" Dorothea asked perplexedly. "Aren't building permits a matter for the local council?"

"Unfortunately Seamus Trevinion is the chairman of the

98

parish council, and our representative on the rural district council," Miss Araminta said drily.

"Who is he? Grace Trevinion's brother?"

I had wondered if my mother's parents were alive. I hadn't thought about any brothers or sisters of hers. It was odd to realize that I might have uncles and aunts and cousins here.

"No, the only son was killed in the war; Seamus was his cousin. According to rumor, he was the man her parents wanted Grace to marry," Miss Araminta told me. "He runs the estate for old Mrs. Trevinion. She has been a widow for ten years. The younger Mrs. Trevinion, her widowed daughter-in-law, Monica, lives with her. Also her grandchildren, her older daughter's twins. A wild pair of youngsters—"

"Quite a family," I commented, with a mixture of excitement and apprehension.

It was something of a shock to realize that I had so many unknown relatives. Would I have the nerve to introduce myself to them? I would like to see my grandmother, but what of the others? They were unlikely to welcome me, and I probably would have very little in common with them. My background and upbringing were probably vastly different from theirs.

"Sit down, my dears! No sense in waiting for Adam," Miss Araminta said briskly. "It's only Irish stew, but it'll put some warmth into you. It's chilly tonight."

The stew tasted as good as it smelled. It was a real old-fashioned Irish stew with potatoes, turnips, carrots, onions and celery cooked with steak and dumplings in a rich gravy. I discovered, as I tackled my generous plateful, that I was hungry. Dorothea, who usually had the naturally hearty appetite of a student, didn't seem to be making much progress with her portion though.

"What's the matter, dear? Don't you care for stew?" Miss Araminta asked in concern. "Would you rather have some eggs?"

"Oh, no thank you! This stew's very good," Dorothea responded hurriedly. "I'm just not hungry."

"Tell us some more about the Trevinions, Miss Denver," I

said impulsively. "Is the manor that house set among the trees on the far side of the creek?"

She nodded. "It seems strange that you don't know anything about the family. You must be Mrs. Trevinion's granddaughter, and the twins must be your cousins. You'll really be a shock to them," she said bluntly. "They behave as though they own the place already. It's not entailed though, so maybe Seamus Trevinion will inherit it."

"Lyra doesn't belong to the Trevinions; she belongs to us," Dorothea said abruptly, as if daring Miss Araminta to contradict her. "Grace Trevinion gave her to my mother, and my father legally adopted her; the Trevinions can't take her away from us."

"Of course not," I said. Again, I was warmed by Dorothea's insistence. "There's no reason why they should even try."

If I had been cherishing a vague, sentimental picture of elderly, lonely grandparents, yearning for their lost daughter and her offspring, it had been dispelled by what Miss Araminta had told us. My grandmother appeared to have plenty of company at the manor; the formidable Seamus, whom no doubt she regarded as a son, a widowed daughter-in-law, and twin grandchildren. Probably it was a close-knit family circle in which there would be no place for me even if I had coveted one.

"You wanted to see them," Dorothea reminded me.

"Yes. At least, I would like to see the old lady—to set her mind at rest about her daughter. She must have worried if she never had any news of Grace."

"From all I've heard, she was furiously angry rather than worried." Miss Araminta was gazing at me in a way which I couldn't interpret. "If you're anticipating a frail, sweet, white-haired old lady, you're in for a shock, child. Mrs. Trevinion looks and acts younger than her own daughter-in-law. She has amazing vitality. As a girl she was a spoiled and lovely and headstrong heiress. She hasn't mellowed with the years. I've been told that she bitterly resented and opposed Adam's appointment to this parish."

"Why?" I asked in perplexity.

"Nobody appears to know how her feud against the church began—or why. I understand that she never enters St. Petroc's except for a family wedding or funeral, and she is directly responsible for keeping her family away too."

"How extraordinary!" I said blankly. "She can't want her grandchildren to grow up without any faith. Are they orphans?"

"Yes. Their parents were killed in a car accident when they were small children."

"How old are they now?" I asked.

"Seventeen. They both left their boarding schools last July."

"That's very early to leave school," Dorothea observed disapprovingly.

"Yes. I heard that the grandmother was asked to remove Jay, the boy, and his sister refused to stay at school if he was to be at home." Miss Araminta's brows puckered. "I'm afraid they'll be a sore trial to us. When we were moving in, the girl, Kay, fairly haunted us. She tried to flirt with Adam, silly child, and obviously resented it when he refused to play up to her."

I bit my lower lip hard. It was ridiculous to feel protective over a man I had only just met, but I was swept by a surge of anger toward my unknown cousin. Did it appeal to her sense of humor to pester the young vicar? She must be well aware of her grandmother's attitude toward him. Was she deliberately trying to embarrass Adam? He might find it difficult to rebuff her, but she would have me to reckon with now.

9

ADAM RETURNED when we were finishing our supper with cake and coffee. He had changed into dark gray flannel trousers and a dark jacket for his visit to the stricken old lady. The somber clothes made him look older, or maybe it was his grave, abstracted expression which had momentarily obliterated that impression of boyishness.

We were seated around the old range. Miss Araminta had explained apologetically that they had opened up the drawing room but hadn't yet lighted a fire in the grate, so the room was chilly. There was an oil stove in the smaller room which Adam used as a study, but she found it cozier to sit in the kitchen.

"How is Mrs. Williams?" his aunt inquired. "Still conscious?"

"Oh, yes! She's holding her own, and she seemed pleased to see me," Adam answered. "Monica Trevinion was with her. Genuinely concerned about her."

"That's surprising! I wouldn't have guessed that visiting the sick was in Monica Trevinion's line," Miss Araminta said bluntly.

"It's a mistake to jump to conclusions," Adam said in mild rebuke. "Mrs. Williams was housekeeper at the manor when Monica came there as a young bride, and I could see there's real affection between them. Monica was on the verge of tears and the dear old lady was trying to console her."

"Amazing!" Miss Araminta declared. "That young woman looks and acts as if she were incapable of any natural emotion. Cool as glass but much less transparent."

"A deeply unhappy woman, unless I'm very wrong about her," Adam said slowly but with conviction. "That chilly façade seemed to have cracked tonight. I felt that her hostility toward me was entirely impersonal—simply a habit."

"Hostility?" I echoed.

He turned to look at me, and the gravity of his expression seemed to lighten. Our eyes met, and again it was as though we were recognizing and greeting each other as old friends.

"Yes. When the district nurse arrived to get Mrs. Williams ready for the night, and we were leaving the cottage, Monica Trevinion let me have it. She accused me of frightening the patient by 'coming to pray over her,' as she called it, and demanded what good I imagined my prayers could do. She said Martha Williams was the last person who needed praying for and I had a nerve to inflict myself on her when she was ill and helpless." His tone was even, but I thought I detected a hurt note beneath it. "I assured her that Mrs. Williams had sent for me, and she looked at me with bitter resentment. Then she said abruptly, 'I suppose you're just another well-meaning fool. Prayers never help anyone. I know; I used to pray—years ago. It was a sickening waste of time and effort.' "

"Perhaps she was thinking of her husband. Your aunt said he was killed in the war. If Mrs. Trevinion had been praying for his safety, she might have felt that her prayers had gone unheard," I said impulsively. "To some women, only their own personal loss seems real or important."

"Could be," Adam agreed. "But, that was over twenty years ago. That's a long time to harbor such bitterness. Then, she said, 'You look like a strong young man. Why don't you find yourself a real job of work instead of harassing sick old people?' in a witheringly contemptuous tone—"

It had been that taunt which had stung him, I realized with a rush of compassion toward him. I longed to say something inspiring and comforting, but no words came to me. I could only look at him and, in a strange way, feel his hurt as if it were my own.

It was Dorothea who broke the silence. "Father used to have to face that kind of sneer when he was younger," she said. "During the war particularly, while he was the vicar of a country parish in Devon, people would accuse him of taking cover in a safe place instead of facing his country's enemies. He felt it acutely. He had applied for a service chaplaincy and been turned down because he was very subject to asthma and bronchitis when he was young."

"Oh?" I said in surprise. "I didn't know that."

"He never talked about it for fear of distressing Mother. She couldn't stand for him to be hurt. Aunt Clara told me," Dorothea said hurriedly. "Mother thought it was for her sake —and yours—that he stayed in Devon. So did his friends. Scarcely anyone realized that in any big city he was liable to be laid low by asthma."

"That must have been tough for him," Adam said with feeling.

"It was, because he's a big man and always looked physically fit. And he was never afraid," Dorothea said warmly. "To be suspected of cowardice stung his pride badly."

"He weathered it?"

"Oh, yes! My aunt said she used to remind him that Christian soldiers are always in the firing line. Plenty of them, like Father, would rather face bullets and bombs then hurtful taunts, but they're not always given the option." She paused, blushing, and I guessed that she was thinking of herself as well as of Father. Hadn't she admitted that she had suffered at school when tactless teachers had compared her to me? She had the same kind of pride as Father. Though she rarely betrayed it, Dorothea cared what people thought of her. That was probably one reason why she had been "such a good child," as Aunt Clara had always remarked. Physically, Dorothea was much braver than I could ever be. But if it were a question of facing adverse criticism, I was tougher.

"That's one for you, my boy," Miss Araminta said with a significant glance at her nephew. "You'd rather face 'sticks

104

and stones' than bitter words. Sit down now and have your supper. No need to let Monica Trevinion upset you; that woman is her own worst enemy."

"In what way?" I asked curiously as Adam seated himself obediently at the table.

"For over twenty years, ever since she lost her husband, she has just been wasting her life. She's fit and active and comparatively young, with no financial anxieties. And what does she do with herself? Nothing! She doesn't need to earn a living, but there's plenty of voluntary work she could tackle," Miss Araminta said bluntly. "I suppose I should be sorry for her, but I'd like to shake her awake to all the opportunities she's missing."

"It certainly sounds like a dreary kind of existence," I said thoughtfully. "Perhaps she's greatly attached to her mother-in-law and couldn't bear to leave her."

"I doubt it," Miss Araminta answered. "Old Mrs. Williams once told me that Mrs. Trevinion had never forgiven her son's wife for not presenting her with a grandson. There was talk at one time that she hoped Monica and Seamus would become interested in each other, but nothing came of it. Apparently they frequently disagree." Miss Araminta set a large plateful of stew in front of Adam and patted him affectionately on the shoulder as if he were still a small boy. "Now get that inside you, and stop fretting. You look as if you've all the cares of the county on your shoulders."

"Of the parish," he amended with a wry smile. "Jim Williams is worried about his crab pots. He says someone's lifting them and taking his crabs and lobsters. He has even found damaged pots substituted for his."

"Jim? That's the older son. He's a sensible, level-headed fellow, and not the type to make unfounded charges," Miss Araminta said with conviction. "Has he any idea who's robbing him?

"He was cagey about naming anyone, but he's badly worried. He says he's having a time making ends meet." Adam's dark brows met. "His wife was less reticent. She said the Trevinions had had their knife in Jim ever since he quit working for them as a gardener and chauffeur. She suspects the twins are playing tricks on him."

"They're a reckless, mischievous pair, but would they go that far?" Miss Araminta demurred. "They must know Jim depends on his crab pots for a living during the off-season when he can't take tourists fishing."

I remembered the shadowy figures I had glimpsed by the creek. They had been loading crab pots into a boat. In the twilight they had looked strangely identical. It could have been the twins, setting out to raid Jim's pots. Or was that just a wild guess?

"Jim had promised to come up and give me a hand with cutting the shrubbery, but now he's getting cold feet," Adam said ruefully. "Apparently Seamus Trevinion took a dim view of Jim's cutting the grass in the churchyard. Told him that if he had time on his hands, there were plenty of jobs which needed tackling in the manor grounds."

"That's typical!" Miss Araminta said indignantly. "Those Trevinions! They act as if they own every living soul in the parish—"

She checked herself abruptly, as if recalling my connection with the Trevinions. I was afraid she would mention it to Adam. Perhaps she would have done so, but Dorothea caused a diversion by rising and glancing at me appealingly.

"Don't you think we should go to bed now, Lyra? It has been a long day, and you're not really well yet," she said jerkily. "If Miss Denver will excuse us—"

"Of course! I'll just run up and light the lamp for you," Miss Araminta said promptly.

I really didn't want to leave the kitchen, and Adam, but I had no excuse for lingering. I longed to make it clear to him that I was here because I had felt impelled to discover something about my mother and her background, not because I was eager to claim kinship with her family. Whatever their attitude toward me might be, if I made myself known to them, I would certainly never ally myself with them against him.

Only, I didn't have any sound reason for believing that what I thought or felt could be important to Adam. It was

106

simply a vague, intangible feeling, as unsubstantial as the gossamer threads of a spider's web, that we were destined to matter to each other. I was aware of him as I had never been aware of any man before, but I couldn't be sure that he was equally aware of me. He had so much else on his mind.

We exchanged brief good-nights, and then Dorothea and I followed Miss Araminta upstairs again. She was lighting our way with a sizable, lantern-shaped flashlight, but its beam only emphasized the darkness of this large old house, and cast eerie shadows on the walls. Dorothea kept close beside me, her hand clutching my arm a little too tightly. That puzzled me. I wouldn't have expected anyone so sane and sensible to be affected by a childish, primitive fear of the dark. Perhaps it was partly her shortsightedness which made her nervous in a poor light.

Even with the lighted lamp and two candles, our bedroom seemed full of shadows. Dorothea, still holding onto me, peered around the big room as if half expecting to see bogeys lurking in the corners.

"The water in the boiler is really hot because I thought Adam would want a bath after cutting the grass," Miss Araminta said briskly. "You can fill your hot-water bottles in the bathroom. Anything else you need? No? Then I'll say good night and God bless."

She beamed at us, then trotted away. Like many plump women, she was quick and light on her feet. As the door closed behind her, Dorothea drew a long breath and released my arm.

"Those people—" she said shakily. "The more we hear about them, the more I wish we hadn't come here. They sound horrible."

"I expect village gossip exaggerates. Don't worry," I tried to reassure her.

"And that man—" She paused uncertainly.

"Seamus Trevinion?"

"No. The vicar."

"Adam? What about him?" I asked defensively.

"You're thinking of him as Adam already, and you don't

know anything about him. You're so terribly impetuous, Lyra. It's no use asking you to be careful, is it?" she said unhappily.

"Careful? Of Adam? Why?" I challenged her.

"This is all my fault. I feel dreadfully guilty," she faltered. "If I hadn't gone to the club with James that night, you and he might have been engaged by now. You wouldn't have gotten involved with Mike, or known about your mother's family, or come here to meet Adam Denver."

"You can't say that. James shied away from me as soon as he learned that I was an adopted daughter. That hurt at the time, but he isn't important any longer," I said firmly. "I was bound to find out about my parents sooner or later. Aunt Clara would inevitably have told me—accident or no accident —and I would have come down here to investigate. Mary would say 'all things work together for good.' We may have been meant to arrive just as this moment."

"For what conceivable reason?"

"Perhaps to throw our weight into the scales."

That could be why Miss Araminta had pressed us to stay here with her and Adam. If she had recognized me instantly as a red-haired Trevinion, she might have seen me as a possible ally. I wasn't likely to have any influence with my unknown relatives, but at least I could do my best to get to the bottom of their inexplicable campaign against the vicar and the church. On the surface, their attitude didn't make sense. Why should they be prejudiced against any and every vicar of their parish?

I was tired enough to fall asleep almost as soon as I snuggled down in bed. Consequently, I woke early. Sunshine was streaming in through the windows and the air felt deliciously fresh. It was going to be a fine day, I decided hopefully, and I didn't want to waste a minute of it.

I was already washed and dressed when a tap on our door heralded Miss Araminta with two cups of tea.

"Had a good night, dear? You're looking a lot better," she said, eyeing me approvingly.

"And feeling it! Thank you for the tea, but you shouldn't have troubled to bring it up to us," I said.

"No trouble. We're early risers. In fact, Adam has already

gone out with Jim Williams to help him haul in his crab pots and long lines. With any luck, we'll have fresh fish for breakfast. That is, if you don't mind waiting till Adam returns."

"Of course not. We'll take a short walk. I'm dying to explore," I assured her.

Dorothea was sitting up in bed brushing her fair hair out of her eyes when I set the tray down between our beds.

"Is it late? Why didn't you wake me?" she asked reproachfully.

"Actually, it's quite early. I hadn't the heart to disturb you. You were sleeping like a child," I told her. "You need a good rest. You've had an anxious time lately, with Mother laid up and all that fuss about Mike's accident."

"I'm glad you realize that I did worry about you. People tend to imagine that I never feel anything," she said resignedly.

We drank our tea in companionable silence. It was odd, I thought again, that now we were better friends and closer to each other than when we had believed we were sisters. Freed from that imaginary bond, we could be friends as we had never been before. Perhaps it was partly because, as the archdeacon's only daughter, Dorothea felt more sure of herself. She could accept me now as I was, instead of being chafed by the difference between us. In fact, she was not only accepting me; she had become very protective over me.

She wouldn't hear of my taking a stroll alone. She insisted that I must wait while she dressed.

"Why on earth?" I was half amused, half vexed. "What do you suppose is likely to happen to me in broad daylight?"

"I don't know, but I promised Mother I would look after you," she persisted. "I'll be quick. Just give me ten minutes."

"Right!" I conceded, guessing that she would be hurt if I didn't wait for her. I perched on the wide windowsill, gazing at the creek and the woods beyond. "There's a fascinating looking path through the trees which I'm dying to explore."

When we reached the bridge over the creek though, Dorothea hung back, protesting. "Those woods are obviously private property. We shouldn't trespass."

"It's a public footpath," I argued, leaning on the worn stone of the bridge and gazing up the creek to the entrance to the path which I had seen from our bedroom window. "Look! There's a notice that says so."

"I can't read it from here. Your sight is amazing," Dorothea said enviously. "Are you sure it's safe? We don't want to be jumped on by any irate landowner."

"Trespassing, unless it's in pursuit of game, or causing willful damage, is no legal offense," I assured her. "Those notices—'Trespassers Will Be Prosecuted'—don't mean a thing."

Still looking reluctant, she followed me down from the bridge to the shore of the creek. The tide was low, and there was a stretch of sticky-looking mud cutting us off from the water. Close to the thick belt of trees though, the ground was sandy and strewn with stones, making firm if uneven walking.

A couple of boats were drawn up above the high-water mark—a light dinghy, and a larger boat with an outboard motor. I suspected that the larger boat was the one I had seen launched last night.

The oaks, beeches and birches were losing their leaves, but they still looked colorful in the sunshine. There were clumps of evergreens among them and tall rhododendrons. When we turned up the path, the towering evergreens seemed to shut out most of the light.

Dorothea stumbled over an exposed root and said uneasily, "I don't like woods; they're so eerie. And it's deathly quiet in here."

"We don't need to go far."

I was reluctant to admit that I was eager for a glimpse of the house in which my mother must have spent her childhood and girlhood. Apparently it hadn't dawned on Dorothea that these woods belonged to the Trevinions, or she would have tried to deter me.

Dead leaves muffled our footsteps. Except for the occasional twitter of a bird, there wasn't a sound to be heard. The trees grew more thickly once we were out of sight of the creek, and the path narrowed as it wound among them.

110

"This path doesn't seem to be leading anywhere. Let's turn back," Dorothea said abruptly.

"Just a little farther," I coaxcd her.

We rounded a bend and were confronted by a high, old-fashioned stile. On either side of it, a stout wire fence had been erected. I wondered why. Surely no cattle or sheep would be grazing in such thick woods. I hopped over the stile and turned to give Dorothea a hand. She climbed awkwardly onto the top bar, hampered by her overly long and rather tight gray flannel skirt. She had one leg over the bar and was reaching for my outstretched hand when there was a sudden explosion, as from a gun, followed almost instantly by another, and the whirr of wings.

Dorothea started violently, and lost her precarious balance. Before I could grab her, she had pitched down headlong. She fell awkwardly, one leg twisted under her. She gave a little cry of pain as I tried to help her to her feet.

"What's wrong? Have you hurt yourself?" I asked anxiously.

She sat up, wincing, and clutching one foot.

"My ankle—" she gasped. "I think I've twisted it."

A dog barked somewhere close at hand, and there was a rustling and crackling among the rhododendrons. Then the dog—a large golden retriever—came bounding up to us. Dorothea cried out in alarm as he attempted to nuzzle her. She had always been afraid of dogs. She flipped at him with both hands and he began to bark loudly. His tail was wagging though and he looked friendly enough, so I caught him by his collar and held him away from her.

The bushes rustled even more violently, and a man stepped out from them onto the path.

"Who the devil are you? And what are you doing here?" he demanded. "Quiet, Bruce! Sit!"

I let go of the dog's collar and turned to gaze up at his owner. He was a very large man in a shabby tweed jacket and corduroy trousers. He had a shotgun under one arm and a brace of dead pheasants in his hand. He looked like a tough, formidable character as he glowered down at Dorothea.

"We were just taking a walk. Your shots startled my sister and she fell off the stile," I answered briefly. "I'm afraid she has sprained her ankle."

"You were lucky not to get a few shots in you," he said unsympathetically. "You have no business wandering in these woods."

"It's a public footpath, and you've no business shooting so close to it," I flashed.

He switched his attention to me at that, his swarthy, heavy-featured face scowling. Then, as our eyes met, his expression changed abruptly. He stared at me as if I were a ghost.

"Grace—" he said on a startled note. "*Grace!* I always knew you would come home in the end—"

He took a couple of steps toward me, then checked himself.

"No, it isn't possible," he said incredulously. "You can't be. You're just a girl."

I caught my breath sharply. At first sight, I had taken him for a gamekeeper. Now I realized that he must be the formidable Seamus Trevinion, the man my mother's parents had wanted her to marry.

He reached out and gripped my wrist none too gently.

"Who are you?" he demanded, giving me a little shake. "Answer me!"

"Don't touch her! Leave her alone. There's—there's blood on your hand," Dorothea cried out raggedly. "Lyra, please, help me up and let's get away from here."

I jerked my wrist free. It was true that his fingers were stained with the blood of the pheasants which he had dropped when he had grabbed me. His rough clasp had left a smear on my skin, I noticed. I bent to rub it off on the moss on which Dorothea had landed. Then I put my hands under her shoulders and hauled her to her feet. She clung to me, flinching, and white with pain. Already her ankle appeared to be swelling, and it was obvious that she couldn't walk back to the vicarage.

I had never felt more helpless. I blamed myself for the curiosity which had prompted me to follow this lonely path.

112

What in the world were we to do now? I could hardly carry Dorothea back to the road.

"I'll have to get to a phone and call Adam. I suppose he has a car. You can't walk with that sprained ankle," I said ruefully.

"Adam?" Seamus echoed sharply.

"Adam Denver. We're staying at the vicarage," I explained hurriedly. "Where is the nearest telephone?"

"At the house. We'd better take her there; it isn't far," he said shortly. "Hold my gun, and I'll carry her."

"Is it loaded?" I asked apprehensively.

With an impatient gesture, he snapped the gun open, removed two cartridges and pocketed them. Then he closed the gun and handed it to me.

"Lyra—" Dorothea was leaning heavily on me and there were beads of perspiration on her forehead and upper lip, but she jerked up her chin defiantly. "I don't want to go to the house; I'll wait here while you contact the vicar."

Seamus had said "the house" as if it were written in capital letters. Dorothea said it in the same way but with a kind of horror in her tone, as if she were speaking of a monster's castle.

"Don't be silly, girl! That ankle needs attention," Seamus said roughly, making a purposeful move toward her.

"No! You're Mr. Trevinion, aren't you? Leave me alone."

She shrank away from him awkwardly and put her weight on her injured ankle. She gave a stifled gasp of pain, and the color drained from her cheeks. If I hadn't still had one arm around her, she would have fallen. She swayed and her head came to rest limply on my shoulder.

"Confound her! Now she has blacked out on us," Seamus said irritably. "Here! I'll take her."

He seized Dorothea and swung her up, over his shoulder, as if she had been a child. I didn't echo her protest. Although I didn't want to be marched up to "the house" either, I couldn't see any alternative. I couldn't leave her here in a near-fainting condition while I went for help. Someone would obviously have to carry her back to the road, and Adam might still be

113

out with the fisherman. I could phone James at the inn, of course, but he would fuss and fret and make a great production of coming to our rescue. Furthermore, he wouldn't know where to find us and it would be difficult to explain. Besides, James wasn't built for carrying a girl who was nearly as large as himself. Dorothea was slim, but she was tall and big-boned.

I said confusedly, "Thank you! I'm very sorry to trouble you, but it really was your fault for startling my sister with those shots."

"Let's not waste breath fighting about who's to blame," he said curtly. "Heel, Bruce!"

He set off with a firm, purposeful stride up the path, the dog at his heels. I glanced at the dead birds lying on the ground, but I couldn't bring myself to pick them up. Shouldering the heavy shotgun, I followed Seamus, trying to brace myself for what lay ahead.

10

I WILL NEVER FORGET my first sight of the manor. The path emerged from the woods onto a broad graveled drive, and there was the house—its gray stone walls covered with a riot of colorful Virginia creepers, and a row of evergreens forming a dark background. With its turret windows and twin towers and twisted chimneys, it looked like something out of a fairy tale.

I realized vaguely that architecturally it was a weird mixture of periods, but time had blended the conflicting styles into an impressive whole. Below a wide terrace, on which massed chrysanthemums made a glowing ribbon of color against the stone balustrade, there was a large rose garden. In this sheltered position, there were still roses in bloom, and I imagined I could detect their fragrance as we passed them.

I had been following Seamus and the retriever up the narrow path. Now, in the wide drive, he paused and glanced back at me.

"Well?" he jerked out abruptly. "Isn't it time you explained who you are—and what you're doing here?"

"I'm Lyra Haughton, and this is my sister, Dorothea. We're staying at the vicarage for the weekend," I answered tentatively.

"Which tells me precisely nothing. Where did you come from, and what do you want here?" he demanded.

His eyes, steely gray and deep set beneath heavy grizzled eyebrows, seemed to rake my face. I forced myself to look back at him steadily. It was strange to realize that this man might have been my mother's husband. Like the house, he was impressive looking, with his powerfully built figure and bold, craggy features, but the steely glint in his eyes and the hard line of his lips repelled me. I sensed intuitively that he would be a dangerous enemy. There was a strong suggestion of the autocrat about him, as if he were accustomed to having his word regarded as law.

"We live in Kelchester," I said evenly. "We came down to Port Petroc for a quiet weekend."

"Who are you trying to fool? Except for your eyes, you might be Grace Trevinion—as she was twenty-five years ago. You must be her daughter; there's no other possible explanation for such a remarkable likeness," he said forcefully. "Did she send you here?"

"Nobody sent me." With that penetrating glance on me, I knew it would be futile to try to evade his assumption. "I was curious to see Grace Trevinion's old home and to know if any of her family were alive."

"Grace Trevinion?" he echoed sharply. "That's an odd way to speak of your mother."

"I've only recently discovered that she was my mother," I said frankly. "I can't think of her as my mother."

Dorothea had been lying limply across his shoulder, her eyes closed. She gave a sudden jerk and flinched. Her eyes opened and sought mine compellingly.

"She wasn't. My mother has been Lyra's mother ever since Lyra was a tiny baby," she said feverishly. "Lyra belongs to us. Isn't that true, Lyra?"

"Certainly. I was legally adopted."

"Did that plausible swine of a parson abandon Grace and her baby?" Seamus exploded. "Why didn't she come home? She knew I would have married her no matter what she had done."

116

"Very generous of you, but she already had a husband," I said, indignant at the implied slur on my unknown father. "He was killed in an air raid."

"Grace should have come home. She never even wrote to us." His voice sounded as if he was having difficulty suppressing strong emotion. "She always was stubborn; and after she became so religious, she wouldn't listen to any of us. Where is she now? Did she marry again?"

"No. She died when I was a baby."

"She's *dead?*"

It was as though an east wind had swept over his rocklike features. There was a chilling bleakness in his eyes, and his mouth seemed to tighten and harden. In a stony silence, he quickened his strides. I knew then that, however she had felt about him, he had loved Grace Trevinion and gone on hoping that some day she would return to the manor.

I almost had to run to keep up with him as he swung past the terrace to what was evidently the main door of the house. It was a massive oak door, standing half open. As he proceeded up the wide marble steps which led up to it, a girl came out onto the steps; she was a slender, black-haired girl in a thick sweater and tight stretch nylon slacks. She stopped short, staring at us.

"Hello! I heard the shots. Did you hit someone, Seamus?" she inquired with an impish grin. "I knew you would some day."

"This young woman tripped over the stile and hurt her ankle. Call your aunt!" he said brusquely.

The girl darted back, and he carried Dorothea into a large, high-domed hall. He lowered her onto an oak settee, as if dislodging a sack of potatoes from his shoulder. Seeing a spasm of pain cross Dorothea's blanched face, I thrust the gun into his hands and dropped down beside her, putting an arm around her protectively.

Seamus straightened himself and glowered down at us balefully.

"Sisters, are you? A pretty pair! Come to claim Grace's inheritance, I presume?" he said scathingly.

"Your presumption is absolutely wrong, Mr. Trevinion," I retorted hotly. "The sooner we're out of this house, the better pleased we shall be."

"So, you've inherited Grace's temper as well as her lovely face and glorious hair?" he said sardonically. "Not her honesty though. You can't convince me that you're not here for what you can get out of us."

"Then I won't waste my time trying," I flashed. "If you'll be good enough to phone the vicarage, I'm sure Mr. Denver will come for us."

"I don't doubt it. A lot of that young parson's problems would be solved if he could latch onto a Trevinion, and he's shrewd enough to know it," he said grimly. "Brought you down here to harass us, did he?"

"Certainly not. We'd never even seen the Denvers till we arrived here last night. And don't talk to my sister in that tone," Dorothea interposed indignantly. "She doesn't want anything from you. Grace Trevinion gave her to my parents, and my father, Archdeacon Haughton, adopted her."

"An archdeacon! Don't tell me that she's inherited her mother's religious mania?" he said derisively. "That would hardly fit in with her descent on us to cash in on Grace's share of the family fortune."

Before I could think of a crushing retort, the black-haired girl came darting across the hall, followed by a tall, fair woman.

"What is all this, Seamus?" the woman demanded imperiously. "Kay says you shot a girl on the stile. Is she badly hurt?"

"Nothing of the sort. The girl fell off the stile and seems to have sprained her ankle," he said curtly. "Would you take a look at it, Monica?"

So this was Monica Trevinion. I eyed her in frank curiosity. She would have been a strikingly attractive woman if it hadn't been for her cold, withdrawn expression.

"Really, Kay—" she said, glancing at her young niece in chilly disapproval. "Your exaggerations!"

"It made a better story that way," Kay answered, grinning

impenitently. "Besides, with his thing about trespassers, Seamus is quite capable of taking potshots at them."

"Horrible kid!" Seamus grunted, but there was a softened, indulgent look on his harsh features as Kay twinkled up at him.

Monica's tone was considerably less affectionate as, having bent down to inspect Dorothea's swelling ankle, she ordered Kay to get a basin of cold water, antiseptic and bandages.

"I'll put a cold compress on the ankle, but I'd advise you to let the doctor examine it. You may have to have it bandaged," she said crisply. "It looks like quite a bad sprain. Painful?"

Dorothea nodded, and I said, "It was painful enough to make her faint when she tried to stand on that foot."

"I didn't think girls went in for sprained ankles these days. It's like a Jane Austin heroine," Seamus observed cynically. "A sprained ankle and a faint! I can't see Kay going in for either."

"Oh, Kay!" Monica's thin lips tightened. "She's as tough as her twin, and just as tiresome. You shouldn't encourage her, Seamus."

"You don't have to talk as if we'd deliberately staged my sister's fall," I burst out, resenting the skeptical glint in his eyes.

"Sure you didn't? It would be one way of gaining admittance to this house," he drawled. "Take a good look at this redhead, Monica. Ever seen her before?

Monica was on her knees removing Dorothea's shoe and stocking. She had nice long hands with pointed fingertips, I noticed. They were smooth and white, as if unused to any manual work, but their movements were deft and surprisingly gentle. Even so, I could feel Dorothea flinching as she leaned against me.

At Seamus' demand, Monica glanced up at me in a cold, dispassionate fashion.

"Who are these girls, and why should I be expected to know them?" she asked impatiently.

"You don't recognize her?"

She shook her smooth, fair head. "I've never seen her

before," she said decisively. "They're both strangers to me. They're here on a holiday, surely. Local girls would know better than to wander in our woods; even poachers never enter them since you shot that Penrose boy's dog."

"You never notice anything," Seamus said irritably. "You appear to live in a world of your own."

A faint color stained her clear fair skin at that, and her lips tightened again. I recalled what Miss Araminta had said about the older Mrs. Trevinion's hope that Monica and Seamus might console each other for their lost loves. I sensed that it had been Seamus, not Monica, who had rejected that plan. Monica was obviously far from indifferent to him.

Clad in an immaculate gray sweater set and a heather-colored tweed skirt, a single strand of obviously real pearls at her throat and with her sleekly styled hair and discreetly pale makeup, Monica had a poise and elegance any young girl might have envied. She looked the epitome of cool self-possession. Yet, to Seamus, she was as vulnerable as Dorothea was to James, I thought with reluctant compassion. She might keep the rest of the world at a distance, but his light barb had penetrated her armor.

Kay came back with a bowl of water, a towel, a cloth and bandages.

"Like me to give first aid, Aunt Monica?" she inquired. "I'm quite good at it."

"You? I wouldn't trust you to put a band-aid on a cut finger," Monica retorted crushingly.

It was Kay's turn to blush. She gave her aunt a resentful glance; then she threw back her long dark hair in a defiant gesture.

"Have it your own way! You don't think anyone except yourself can do anything," she muttered. "You have to run everything and everyone—you and Seamus. Jay and I might as well still be in the nursery—"

"That's enough!" Seamus cut her short authoritatively. "Let's see if you have any more perception than your aunt displays. Take a long look at our red-haired trespasser, and tell me if you recognize her."

120

Thus admonished, Kay put her head on one side like an alert terrier and scrutinized me with a terrier's bright, hazel brown eyes.

"Yes!" she said on a startled note. "She's the living image of Aunt Grace."

Monica had her head bent, and was applying the wet cloth to Dorothea's ankle. She started, as if she had received an electric shock.

"Grace?" she echoed. She sat back on her heels, the cloth dripping unheeded onto the beautiful old parquet floor. "Your runaway sweetheart?"

Seamus ignored her and gave Kay an affectionate pat on the back.

"Good for you, Kay! You're right on target," he said approvingly. "Your Aunt Grace is dead, but she left us a daughter."

"Goodness!" Kay was staring at me in unconcealed curiosity. "You're Aunt Grace's daughter? Then we must be cousins. How jolly! Are you a Grace too?"

"No, Lyra. At least, I was christened Lyra Grace, but I've always been called Lyra," I answered. "I'm Lyra Haughton, and my sister is Dorothea."

"Lyra? That's unusual! I'm Kay, as you've probably gathered. After Queen Katherine; that's what we call our grandmother. She won't be called Granny; that dates her." She gave a sudden mischievous chuckle. "She must be your grandmother too, and you're years older than we are. She won't like that."

"Grace's daughter?" Monica said in a startled, horrified tone. "Are you sure, Seamus? Has she papers to prove her claim? She could be an impostor."

"She doesn't need any papers to convince me. Except for her green eyes, she might be Grace; the likeness is quite staggering," Seamus said positively.

"I can imagine that it has rocked you." Monica's tone was as bleak as her expression. "You've never gotten over your sentimental attachment to Grace; you're still carrying a torch for her. But she never cared two cents about you, from all I've heard. She was madly in love with that hot gospel curate."

"Suppose you get on with the job and let the past remain buried," Seamus said harshly. "Grace is dead; leave her memory in peace. You can stop resenting her now."

Monica's color deepened. Her narrow, blue-gray eyes were like slivers of ice as she looked up at me.

"Your mother may be dead, but this whole house and all our lives are haunted by her. We're never allowed to forget her or her brother, who was my husband," she said bitterly. "She has done us enough harm. Why have you come here to add to it?"

"I'm sorry," I said, shocked by her tone. "Perhaps I shouldn't have come. It was just curiosity—"

"We're not staying. We're going home on Monday," Dorothea said quickly.

Kay looked at her in a puzzled fashion. "Are you a cousin too? Nobody would take you for sisters."

"Dorothea's parents adopted me when I was a baby. Before she was born," I explained. "I was an orphan."

"You were adopted? How weird!" Kay said blankly. "I mean, why weren't you sent here to Queen Katherine and Grandfather? They would have doted on you."

"Lyra's mother didn't want her to be brought up here," Dorothea answered for me. "She said this wasn't a Christian home."

"Well! For crying out loud!" Kay ejaculated. "That sounds as if Aunt Grace really did suffer from religious mania. Are you that way too?"

"Grace was right at that. There's nothing Christian about this ill-assorted household," Monica said coldly. "Mrs. Trevinion is against any form of religion, and that's putting it mildly. If you girls are what's called professing Christians, you'd better hurry back to the vicarage before you become contaminated."

Dorothea blushed, but she said steadily, "Yes. That's what we intend to do."

"Queen Katherine may have something to say about that,"

122

Seamus interposed. "Who should break the news to her? Any offers? No? Then I guess it's up to me."

"You're the one who appears to be sponsoring this girl's claim," Monica reminded him. "I never knew Grace. I certainly wouldn't consider myself qualified to recognize her daughter."

He nodded curtly and strode away, crossing the hall to the double staircase at the far end. He went up the stairs with a slow, heavy tread, like the pounding of my heartbeats. I had a sudden, wild longing to escape. I didn't, after all, want to meet my unknown grandmother. I didn't want to be involved in any way with what Monica had called "this ill-assorted household." I think I might have yielded to that strong impulse to flee, but I couldn't abandon Dorothea. Her fingers were digging into mine, as if to brace herself to endure the pain in her ankle.

Monica, her face like marble, was bandaging the ankle now, her hands moving swiftly, as if she was eager to finish the task and get us out of the house.

Evidently the same thought had crossed Kay's mind, because she said, "You needn't hurry, Aunt Monica. Queen Katherine isn't likely to be down just yet."

Monica made no response to that, and Kay turned to me, explaining: "Our gay young grandmother was out late last night, at one of her interminable bridge parties."

"Oh? You were out late too, weren't you? In your boat," I responded.

"How did you know? Were you spying on us?" Kay demanded.

"I saw you from our bedroom window. With some crab pots."

"Kay!" Monica had secured the bandage. She rose and eyed her niece frostily. "You haven't been raiding Jim Williams' pots again? How could you, when his mother's dying?"

"Old Martha won't conk out just yet. She's too tough," Kay retorted flippantly. "Harassing the godly is about the only amusement left to us since Queen Katherine confiscated Jay's car. What's wrong with it? Are you developing a conscience or something, Aunt Monica?"

"Don't be impertinent!" Monica said frostily. "To take that fisherman's catch is just plain stealing."

"Oh, but we don't!" Kay protested. "We don't want his crabs and lobsters. We just turn them loose."

"Why?" I asked directly.

"Just to teach him a lesson—him and old holier-than-thou Martha," she answered defiantly. "They had the nerve to complain to the police about Jay's driving, and the police set a trap for us. Poor Jay was arrested for speeding in the village, and they took his license. What do you think of that?"

"I think it's very dangerous to drive fast through these narrow lanes," I said frankly.

"Jay got what he deserved. He sent old Mrs. Williams flying. She might have been killed instead of merely bruised and shaken," Monica said severely.

"She came teetering out of her cottage without looking where she was going," Kay said defiantly. "Anyway, he didn't deserve to have his car confiscated; that was terribly unfair. It wasn't because Queen Katherine cared whether he killed any of the villagers or not. It was just because she was afraid he might smash up himself or me. As if he would! He's a jolly fine driver."

"Typical!" Monica said, with a brittle, mirthless laugh. "I'm afraid you're shocking your new cousin, Kay. She evidently hasn't been brought up in the Trevinion philosophy—that it couldn't matter less what happens to the rest of the world, provided that the Trevinions can have their own sweet way."

"Why should we care about anyone else? Nobody cares about us," Kay said with a tilt of her chin. "Most of the villagers loathe the lot of us, though most of 'em are too scared to show it."

"You're not likely to endear yourselves to the local inhabitants by filching their fish or running down their old ladies," I said mildly.

"You shouldn't preach! If your mother hadn't run away and our uncle and my parents hadn't been killed, Queen

Katherine wouldn't have kept us on such a tight rein," Kay flared. "She can't bear to have us out of her sight. I wanted to train as a nurse and Jay wanted to be a vet, but we didn't have a hope! She lost all her children, and she's determined to keep her grandchildren safe here, right under her thumb."

"A nurse? *You?*" Monica said scathingly. "Nursing means hard work; you wouldn't stick to it for a week. You've never done anything in your life except amuse yourself."

"What else is worth doing? Are you at it again, Kay?" a light, assured tenor voice asked. "What's going on around here? Isn't anyone having breakfast this morning?"

It was easy to see that the young man who was sauntering toward us was Kay's twin. He had the same nearly black hair, hazel brown eyes and slight build. In contrast with Seamus and Monica, the twins looked very young and unsure of themselves beneath their surface air of bravado. Kay had applied eye shadow and eye liner with a lavish hand, but they merely emphasized the immaturity of her features.

Both twins seemed years younger than Dorothea too. Dorothea could be clumsy and awkward, but basically she was already a responsible adult. She had her course in life chartered and knew where she was going, and she had the courage of her convictions. She was vastly more mature than Kay, who conveyed the impression of drifting, rudderless and anchorless, on a stormy sea.

"So—that's where you've been? Stuffing yourself, and missing all the excitement." Kay hailed her twin. "Just look what Seamus has brought in from the woods! Meet Cousin Lyra Haughton and her adopted sister."

"*Cousin?*" Jay echoed with a quirk of his brows.

"Aunt Grace's daughter. Seamus is thrilled to bits with her, but Aunt Monica's gnashing her teeth," Kay said lightly. "Personally, I haven't made up my mind about her yet. She seems on the pious side, but she may take the heat off us."

"Depends on Queen Katherine's reaction. She has never forgiven her truant daughter for eluding her clutches," Jay said reflectively.

"And never ceased to tell us how wonderful Aunt Grace

was, either, and how different everything would have been here if she hadn't let herself be deluded and led astray by a handsome, plausible curate," Kay reminded him. "If you ask me, Queen Katherine will grab Aunt Grace's daughter with both hands. Seamus will too. Perhaps he'll fall in love with her."

"Really, Kay! Can't you learn to think before you rattle on in that ridiculous fashion? You're embarrassing your cousin," Monica interposed coldly. "You're talking of her parents."

"Sorry!" Kay had the grace to look abashed. "Only, they've been family legends so long that I can't see them as real people. I mean, it was like one of those old-fashioned romantic novels—the lovely daughter of the manor and the penniless parson with his gift of the gab who converted her and married her."

It was odd and disconcerting to realize that these Trevinions knew so much more about my parents than I did. To me, they weren't even legends. I had begun to form a picture of my mother, but my father remained an unknown, shadowy figure.

"What happened to them? Are they on the rocks financially? Is that why they've sent you here?" Jay inquired cynically. "Welcome, anyway, cousin, and the best of luck! You'll find Queen Katherine holds onto the purse strings with grim determination."

"How do you do?" I said, trying to rein in my rising temper. "You Trevinions appear to have singularly suspicious minds. Aren't you rather young to be such a cynic? For the record, my parents died many years ago. My foster parents are certainly not 'on the rocks,' as you call it."

"How was I to know?" Jay looked boyishly embarrassed, and I realized that his cynicism, like Kay's rebelliousness, was mainly a pose. "I can't see why anyone would venture into this open prison unless it was in the hope of getting some dough out of Queen Katherine."

"That's a nice, grateful attitude to adopt after all your grandmother has done for the pair of you," Monica said censoriously. "You're both thoroughly spoiled, and your manners are utterly deplorable."

126

"We follow the example set for us by our elders and betters." Kay grinned. "What about offering our long-lost cousin and her sister some breakfast? I'm starving."

"Thank you, but we're expected back at the vicarage," I said hurriedly. "If I could phone the Denvers—"

"You can't go till you've been inspected by our formidable grandmother," Kay cut me short. "Come and have some coffee, anyway, to fortify you for the ordeal. If we give Dorothea an arm, she ought to be able to hobble as far as the breakfast room. She looks as if she needs something to revive her."

It was true that Dorothea was still very pale and I sensed that her ankle was paining her in spite of Monica's ministrations. A hot drink would do us both good, I decided, and it was obvious that we weren't going to be allowed to contact the Denvers until we had met the older Mrs. Trevinion.

"Thank you! Coffee would be fine," I answered, and between us, Kay and I helped Dorothea to her feet.

11

DOROTHEA MUST HAVE SPRAINED her ankle very badly, I thought anxiously, because she nearly fainted again before we reached the breakfast room. She collapsed into an armchair, looking very sick with pain. Kay, with unexpected kindness, brought a footstool and we propped her injured leg up on it.

I felt terribly guilty. This was supposed to be Dorothea's midterm holiday, and she had been looking forward to our trip. Now, by my curiosity and impetuosity, I had ruined it for her. It was obvious that she would have to lie in bed instead of exploring the neighborhood. Apart from the discomfort, she would inevitably feel embarrassed at being incapacitated away from home, in the house of strangers. Miss Araminta and Adam would understand though, I tried to assure myself. I must get Dorothea back to the vicarage as soon as possible.

"Drink this hot coffee," Kay said solicitously, handing Dorothea a fragrant, steaming cupful of coffee. "I'll go and phone our doctor. He'll give you something for the pain."

"Thank you," I said gratefully. "And please phone the vicarage too. The Denvers must be wondering what on earth has become of us."

"James, too. He's probably at the vicarage by now," Dorothea said faintly.

"James? Who's James?" Kay asked curiously.

"The friend who drove us down here from Kelchester. I work in his father's office," I explained. "He's staying at the inn."

"You work in an office? As a typist? That won't go down very well with Queen Katherine," Kay warned me. "Is this James your 'steady'?"

"No, just a friend," I said hastily. "Could you please ask the Denvers to tell him what's delaying us?"

She nodded and skipped away.

From the breakfast table, where she was eating a plateful of bacon and eggs, Monica observed, "You appear to have a full and quite a satisfactory life, Lyra. If you take my advice, you won't give your grandmother a chance to disrupt it."

"Of course not. Why should she try?" I countered.

"Because she's an insanely possessive woman. She owns this estate and seeks to own everyone on it too," Monica answered with leashed bitterness. "As Kay told you, your grandmother controls the Trevinion money. We're all dependent upon her. As long as we go her way, she's generous, even overindulgent, but she doesn't let any of us live our own lives."

"That must be very restricting."

"I'm used to it, but I can see what she's doing to the twins. Think well before you forfeit your independence." She looked across at me with a bleak smile. "That's a disinterested warning, though you may not believe it."

"I do believe it," I assured her, remembering what Adam had said about her inward unhappiness. "I appreciate it, but it wasn't necessary. Even if Mrs. Trevinion invited me to stay here, I couldn't. My home is with my parents and sister."

"Then it's a pity you didn't remain there." She paused, then gave that brittle laugh again. "I mean, for your own sake. For my part, I'm thankful to have all the mystery about your mother cleared up at last. For years Seamus and your grandmother have been waiting and hoping to hear from her. For years I've hated her and dreaded that she might come back to them. If only we had known that she was dead! Why weren't we told?"

"I suppose because she died in a London hospital, as Grace

Amberton. She wouldn't have had any papers with her to connect her with the Trevinions. She left her marriage certificate in a sealed envelope with my foster mother, to be given to me when I was of age—"

I broke off abruptly as the door swung open. I caught my breath sharply. I had subconsciously and irrationally been expecting Katherine Trevinion to look like an older, more formidable edition of her daughter-in-law. Instead, the woman who entered on Seamus' arm looked, at first glance, years younger than Monica. She was small and slender, with hair of so rich a gold and so beautifully waved that it might have been a wig in the window of a hairdresser's salon. Her skin was a delicate pink and white and her eyes were a vivid blue. Monica was handsome, in a chilly, pastel fashion. Kay had striking coloring and the bloom of youth. But this woman put them both in the shade. She was lovely, and yet she didn't look quite real. In her blue woolen suit, the exact shade of her eyes, sheer nylons and high-heeled slippers, she reminded me of an expensive doll.

There was nothing doll-like about the expression in those big blue eyes though, as she scrutinized me. They seemed to light up like sapphires. Her coral-pink lips parted in a dazzling smile. As I rose, she let go of Seamus' arm and made a swoop at me. She clasped me to her, and I felt her cheek, cool and soft and sweetly scented against mine.

"My darling baby's little daughter," she said in a low, husky voice. "Oh, child, why didn't you come home before?"

"Not so little, at that. She tops you by half a foot," Seamus observed sardonically. "And don't forget, she's her father's daughter as well as Grace's."

"That dreadful man!" Katherine Trevinion released me and stepped back, scrutinizing me again. "Oh, but this child is all Grace, except for those green eyes! She's lovely—as lovely as her mother was."

"And probably just as stubborn," Seamus warned her.

She swung around on him with an imperative gesture.

"Go away, Seamus! I won't let you spoil this wonderful moment for me. It's like having my darling Grace home again.

130

And, this time, no ranting young evangelist is going to part us. This child will make up for all the heartbreak and suspense Grace inflicted on us," she said emotionally. "If only her grandfather had lived to see her! You know how he adored Grace; nothing was too good for her."

I felt desperately embarrassed. I couldn't look at her. She was demanding so much more than I was prepared to give. I glanced around the room in a hunted fashion. Monica's fair, austere face was registering acute distaste. Dorothea looked worried and apprehensive. Seamus was smiling grimly, as if he was conscious of my discomfort and sardonically amused by it.

"This is Dorothea, Mrs. Trevinion," I said awkwardly. "Her parents adopted me when I was a baby."

"Oh, yes? I hope they looked after you well. We must compensate them for their trouble, of course," Katherine Trevinion said, with a cursory, disinterested glance at Dorothea. "I really can't understand how such an appalling muddle could have occurred. Grace died in a hospital? Then the hospital authorities were to blame. It was their duty to communicate with her parents as soon as they realized that she was seriously ill."

"Apparently, from what Lyra has told us, Grace preferred to hand her baby over to strangers," Monica said dispassionately. "Isn't that so, Lyra?"

"Yes. She chose my mother and father for me. She left me on their porch on Christmas Eve. Mummie accepted me as a Christmas gift, and no mother could have done more for me," I said feelingly. "It was only recently that I learned that I wasn't her own child."

"Illness must have clouded my poor Grace's brain. She couldn't really have thought that her father and I wouldn't have welcomed her child, could she?" Katherine's brilliant blue eyes sought my face in a desperate appeal. "Oh, no! I won't believe that. We loved her so dearly."

I didn't know what to say. I was shaken by conflicting emotions. I had to pity my grandmother, who had lost so much—her husband and all three of her children. It was natural that she should be hurt at my mother's robbing her of her first grandchild. She would be even more hurt if I revealed my mother's reason for having given me to the Haughtons.

Yet, already, I was beginning to understand what had seemed to me inexplicable in the initial shock of learning about my adoption. Grace Trevinion had been determined that her child shouldn't be confined in what Kay, in her extravagant way, had called an "open prison," or reared in what Monica had termed the "Trevinion philosophy." I wasn't to be taught to rely on wealth and privilege; I was to learn from Anne Haughton to value the only "true riches."

"Ye shall know the truth, and the truth shall make you free." That must have been what Grace had discovered and what she had wished for me. It must have taken considerable faith and courage to entrust her baby to strangers, to deliberately abandon all her parents would have lavished on their grandchild, to face the fact that they would find her action unpardonable. Stubborn and fanatical, Grace might have been, but I could think of her with admiration rather than bitterness now.

"It was cruelly hard on you, child, but we'll make it up to you," Katherine Trevinion went on with feverish eagerness. "When her father's anger had cooled, he set up a trust fund for Grace and her children. It has been accumulating for twenty years. Even after you've recompensed your foster parents, you'll have a handsome dowry."

How could I tell her that my parents wouldn't be likely to accept any recompense, or that I didn't want a handsome dowry? Money was obviously of primary importance to her.

To my relief, the door swung open and Kay burst in like a minor rocket. Jay had struck me as a shade lethargic, but Kay seemed to have enough vitality for the pair of them.

"I phoned the vicarage and spoke to our holy man. Your James was with him, so I had a word with him too," she announced breathlessly. "They both sounded a bit on edge. James was all shook up about Dorothea's accident; he's coming up here right away."

"Oh, good!" Dorothea murmured fervently, and Kay gave her a shrewd glance.

"He's your James, not Lyra's, is he? Sorry! I didn't get the picture," she said impishly. "Perhaps he goes for the Jane Austin type. He sounded like a Jane Austin character himself."

"James? Who is James?" Katherine Trevinion demanded, her blue eyes narrowing. "You're not engaged to some man, are you, Lyra?"

"No. James Mallard is a lawyer. The Mallards are family friends of ours. I'm secretary to Walter Mallard, James' father," I explained hastily. "James was kind enough to drive us down here."

"You've been working in an office? Oh, my dear child!" Katherine shook her bright golden head at me in a commiserating fashion. "If only we had known—"

"It's quite a good job and it means that I can live at home," I said defensively.

"At home? This is your home now," she said on a reproachful note, and Kay gave a rippling laugh.

"Have you appropriated Lyra already, Queen Katherine? What do Aunt Monica and Seamus think about that? It's their home too."

"The manor has always been a family home. There's plenty of room for all of you," Katherine answered composedly. She turned to Seamus, who was leaning against the oak-paneled wall, still with that expression of grim amusement. "No doubt you have things to attend to, Seamus. There's no need for you to hang around here. You'll see plenty of your cousin later."

"I just thought you might need some moral support in dealing with the old family friend and our ubiquitous young parson," he drawled. "They both appear to have prior claims to your new granddaughter."

"Nonsense! Don't try to provoke me." She dismissed Seamus with an imperious wave of her hand. "Monica, I won't detain you either. I want to talk to Grace's daughter."

Monica rose without a word and followed Seamus from the room, her thin lips tightly compressed.

"Am I to make myself scarce too?" Kay flashed me a conspiratorial grin. "So long, cousin! You have been warned. I'll bring in the rescue party when he arrives."

The door closed behind her, and Katherine Trevinion seated herself on the settee beside the fire, motioning me to sit beside her. Instead, in a defensive reflex, I perched on the arm of Dorothea's chair. Dorothea gave me a grateful glance and reached for my hand. Katherine's delicately arched brows drew together in a faint frown.

"This is your foster parents' daughter?" she said, surveying Dorothea appraisingly. "From the look of her, they must be respectable people."

"They're very highly respected in Kelchester. Father is Archdeacon Haughton," I said, stung by her patronizing tone. "Mummie is an absolute angel. Dorothea is at the Church of England Training College in Kelchester and doing very well there."

"Indeed? As a family, we severed all connections with the church many years ago. I've no use for parsons of any denomination. Mealymouthed hypocrites—the whole pack of them," Katherine said savagely.

In spite of what the others had told me, that came as a shock, but I bit back the indignant retort on my lips, reminding myself that this was my own grandmother, even though she didn't look like anyone's grandmother.

I said mildly, "That's rather sweeping, Mrs. Trevinion. What grounds have you for your prejudice?"

"Plenty." Her brilliant blue eyes seemed to cloud over, as if at the throb of an old wound. "I was foolish enough to fall in love with a parson when I was Kay's age. I saw him as my ideal—a knight in shining armor. I was all set to marry him until I came up against his bigotry."

"Oh? In what way?"

"He was determined to go to the mission field. Naturally my parents objected. I was a lovely girl, and an heiress. They told him plainly that they would expect him to keep me in comfort, if not in the luxury to which I was accustomed. Though they would have preferred me to do better for myself, my happiness was their main consideration. They were willing to make us a generous allowance and to use their influence to obtain a suitable parish for him."

"And he wouldn't agree to their terms?"

"He threw their generosity back at them. He presented me with an ultimatum: I could come out to Africa with him as his wife and live on his miserable salary, or he would go alone." Her delicate features hardened so that she no longer looked deceptively young. "That was all his so-called love for me was worth. He didn't care how much discomfort I had to endure, provided he could go his own sweet way. A fine Christian!"

"He loved you, but he loved His Master better. If you had loved him enough, you would have understood," Dorothea said earnestly. "A truly dedicated man has to put his calling first."

"Then, may the fates preserve me from such dedication! As, indeed, they did. Soon after he had sailed, Marcus Trevinion proposed to me. He was highly eligible in every way, and my parents were delighted," she said defiantly. "It was a most satisfactory match. I've never lacked anything in my whole life."

"Except love, and a life of service," I said impulsively. "You must have loved that young missionary, or you wouldn't feel so bitter about him."

"I've lacked nothing. My husband adored me till the day he died," she said emphatically. "Service? I was brought up to expect service, not to have to give it. Don't quote your mother to me, child! That was how she talked. And where did it lead her? To a lonely grave."

"No. To 'the joy of her Lord.' That was what she wrote in the letter she left for me. She was happy, Mrs. Trevinion, and she had no fear of death. My father was killed in an air raid and she was ready to join him."

"Pie in the sky." She cut me short contemptuously. "That kind of fairy tale may act as a soothing syrup to children and old women, but you're young and very lovely. You've your life to live, and I'll make sure that you don't throw it away like my poor, misguided Grace. She was a beautiful, spirited youngster, with not a care in the world till she was lured to that wretched mission, and hypnotized by that ginger-haired, green-eyed preacher. Then she seemed to change overnight; it was utterly tragic."

"From your point of view, perhaps. Not from hers. She found joy and peace and a more abundant life. That's quite clear from her letter. You shouldn't regret anything that happened to her," I said, shocked afresh by the savagery of her tone. "She would have died just the same, if she had stayed with you, and she wouldn't have been a believer when she died."

"Nonsense! Her father and I wouldn't have let her die. We would have had the finest specialists in the world for her. No expense would have been spared."

"There are some things money can't buy," Dorothea reminded her.

"Very few, believe me! For instance, with enough money spent on you, child, you could be a beauty, instead of merely nice looking," Katherine pronounced, scrutinizing Dorothea again. "You've a lovely skin and pleasant coloring, but no man would give you a second glance in a crowd. I'll have to get to work on you; I can't bear to see good material wasted."

That brought the color to Dorothea's cheeks and reduced her to an embarrassed silence. She glanced at me helplessly.

"Dorothea only has the weekend off from the college," I said hurriedly. "Her classes begin again on Tuesday."

"With that injured ankle, she won't be back there that soon," Katherine said calmly. "Training to be a schoolteacher, is she? What a waste of energy! Much more profitable to learn to make the most of her looks and find a suitable husband. Anyone can see that she's the marrying kind."

Dorothea gave a stifled gasp and I felt like echoing it. I had supposed her to be set on a successful career; even, perhaps, a natural spinster.

"Oh, yes! I can always tell," Katherine assured us. "She needs a good husband and a couple of babies to bring out the best in her. She'll never make a schoolteacher. She's too diffident. Conscientious, no doubt, but without any flair for

136

managing or disciplining unruly children. A romantic at heart."

"You—you don't know anything about me," Dorothea stammered.

"Probably more than you know about yourself. However, your future isn't my concern. Lyra's is." She flashed a warm, possessive smile at me. "You'll have to marry Seamus, my child. He has been grieving for your mother for years. Now you can make those lost years up to him."

"Oh, Mrs. Trevinion!" I was divided between amusement and exasperation. "Seamus is old enough to be my father!"

"Barely. He was younger than Grace, and he's only forty-three now. In the prime of life. Marry him, and I'll leave the manor to the pair of you. That will solve one of my problems," she said airily.

"What about your other grandchildren and your daughter-in-law?" I began, but she silenced me with an imperative gesture.

"They don't care about the place as Seamus does, but I couldn't leave it to a bachelor. There have always been Trevinions here. The twins don't appreciate that. They're yearning to spread their wings; an ungrateful pair," she said regretfully. "They take after their father. He was the adventurous type—a mining engineer, charming and well bred, but restless. Not really the husband I would have chosen for my older daughter, although he was the son of a baronet. The younger son, unhappily, so he left very little, and we had to use their mother's portion to pay for the twins' education. Kay will have to marry money."

"You can't order people's lives for them," I said helplessly.

She laughed. "Oh, but I can! Very satisfactorily too. I've a suitable husband lined up for Kay already. She's a handful, that child, and an early marriage will be much the best plan for her. I shall have the engagement announced on her eighteenth birthday."

"Is that what she wants?" I asked incredulously.

"She'll come around to it. She won't have any money of her own till she's twenty-one."

Perhaps it was as well that Kay herself reappeared at that point, because I was having difficulty in restraining my indignation at Katherine's sense of values. It wasn't for me to take my grandmother to task, but her whole outlook was utterly alien to mine. It would have horrified Mummie.

"The doctor's here," Kay announced, and stood back for a middle-aged, fatherly looking man to enter the room. "So is James Mallard. You'd better cope with him, Lyra. I'll give the doctor a hand with Dorothea."

12

"THIS IS A REALLY FINE old house. You're in luck, Lyra," James said appreciatively. "Of course, you must stay here as your grandmother insists. Why not?"

"Because I would much rather stay at the vicarage," I said for the third time.

"That's ridiculous! Your whole object in coming down here was to contact the Trevinions. The Denvers are complete strangers. Your grandmother wants you and you can't possibly refuse," James said decisively. "Think of Dorothea, if not of yourself. She'll receive much better care in this house than at the vicarage."

I was in a terrible quandary. I knew that what James was saying made good sense. The doctor had said that Dorothea's ankle was badly sprained, with some injury to the ligaments. He had put it in a cast, advised her to use it as little as possible for the next few days, and given her a sedative.

Katherine Trevinion, as if she realized intuitively that I was vulnerable where Dorothea was concerned, had been sweetly solicitous. She had insisted on Dorothea's being taken upstairs to a guest room and settled down in bed "for a good rest." Dorothea was shocked and shaken, according to the doctor, Katherine had reminded me. Neither she nor the doctor had perceived that the shock was mental rather than physical.

Dorothea was already drowsy from the sedative, and it had been easy for Katherine to sweep aside her faint protests.

I had stayed beside her until she had fallen asleep. Then, reluctantly, I had joined Katherine, James and Monica in the drawing room for coffee. Katherine called it the small drawing room, but it was bigger than any of our rooms at home and beautifully furnished in soft pastel shades. James was obviously impressed by its air of discreet luxury, the thick, pale-hued Persian carpet, the brocade curtains, the delicately upholstered furniture, the hothouse flowers and the Meisson figurines. He was, I feared, even more impressed by Katherine. Monica dispensed coffee and expensive cookies in a cool, withdrawn fashion, but Katherine seemed to be putting herself out to charm and dazzle James.

When she suggested that James should drive me back to the vicarage to get our luggage and make our excuses to the Denvers, James was all for it. Both he and my grandmother obviously thought my hesitation was as ungracious as it was, to them, inexplicable. In Katherine and Monica's presence, I could scarcely voice my real reasons for not wanting to remain here.

"It's most unfitting that my granddaughter should accept hospitality from that tiresome young man and his eccentric aunt," Katherine said with an air of finality. "Haven't I made it clear to you, child, that we don't associate with them? We severed all connections with the parish church years ago when old Mr. Timewell resigned from the parish. The vicars who have succeeded him have been impossible; and this Adam Denver is the worst of the lot."

"In what way?" I demanded.

"So self-assertive and self-opinionated. It's difficult enough as it is to keep him in his proper place," Katherine said severely. "It was most unfortunate that you stayed at the vicarage last night. But, of course, you were unaware of our position. I really can't permit my granddaughter to have any more to do with the Denvers."

I nearly said, "How do you propose to stop her?" but James had risen and was nudging me impatiently.

"Come on, Lyra! You have to pack your things, and it's nearly twelve o'clock. We mustn't keep your grandmother waiting for lunch," he said firmly.

Katherine rewarded him with a gracious smile and an invitation to lunch with us, which he accepted eagerly. There was nothing to do but to let him pilot me out to his car.

"I don't understand you at all. Why this odd sulkiness?" he asked reproachfully as he started the engine. "You ought to be thanking your lucky stars that you've received such a warm welcome from your mother's family. Aren't you thrilled that you come of such stock? Your unknown parents might have been anyone."

"Instead, the Trevinions are really somebody? That's what you mean, isn't it?" I countered. "Don't forget that my mother ran away from them."

"She was young and foolish, and infatuated with that plausible pastor. Your grandmother told me the whole story while you were upstairs with Dorothea."

"She's unfairly prejudiced against my father," I said shortly.

"Not unfairly, from her point of view. The Trevinions are a very old family, and your father was an orphan. He had no idea who his parents were. Apparently he was adopted from an orphanage when he was two years old and brought up by a schoolteacher and his wife."

"Oh? I didn't know that."

"It makes a difference, doesn't it? Your grandmother is very concerned about good breeding. As she said, quite reasonably, the boy wouldn't have been in an orphanage unless his parents had been doubtful characters."

"That's exactly how Father felt about me. Aunt Clara too, even more so. They were always afraid of bad blood coming out in me," I said reflectively. "Strange that the pattern should have repeated itself like that. The Trevinions were afraid of my father's inherited tendencies; your father was afraid of mine."

"Well—" James looked embarrassed. "Natural, wasn't it? Anyway, that's all right now. Father's attitude couldn't alter

141

the way I felt about you, but it seemed unwise to antagonize him."

"Don't you mean inexpedient? You believe in expediency very strongly, don't you?" I said wryly. "You think it's expedient for me now to join forces with the Trevinions and adopt their attitude toward Adam and his aunt?"

"Why not? What are the Denvers to you?" he asked in perplexity.

How was I to answer that? I wasn't sure that I knew the answer. At least, I wasn't until we reached the vicarage. Then, as I entered the shabby hall, I saw Adam at the phone. My heart seemed to give a wild leap. What was Adam to me? More, infinitely more, than all Mike O'Donnell and the Trevinions combined could offer me.

I was Grace's daughter. Perhaps this had happened to me as it had happened to her—this sudden, complete certainty that here was the man with whom I would gladly spend the rest of my life.

"Yes, of course. Come in and see me any evening," Adam was saying. "What? You don't dare come here?—You want me to come to your cottage? That's ridiculous.—As much as your job's worth?—Very well, then! This evening?"

He put down the receiver and swung round, frowning abstractedly. He looked touchingly young and troubled.

"What is it?" I asked impulsively.

"A young couple who want to get married. That was the prospective bridegroom. He says he works on the Trevinion estate and doesn't dare come here openly. It's fantastic!"

"It's like Katherine Trevinion," I said unhappily. "She has this dreadful, savage bitterness toward the church. Adam, what am I to do?"

We stood gazing at each other. I knew from the look in his eyes that I wasn't deceiving myself. Whatever had happened, had happened simultaneously to both of us. He knew it too, whether he was willing to admit it or not.

I was thankful that James had decided to wait for me in his car. He would surely have sensed this strong current of emotion which was sweeping Adam and me together.

142

"About your grandmother?" Adam said soberly. "Aunt Araminta has told me why you're here. From what Kay said on the phone, the Trevinions have accepted you gladly."

"My grandmother has. She's insisting that Dorothea and I must stay at the manor. The Trevinions are my mother's people, but do I have to accept them? The whole atmosphere of that house and their whole outlook upset me," I said desperately. "I don't want anything from them."

"No? Then perhaps there's something they want—or need —from *you*. The bitterness you mentioned—" he said slowly. "Perhaps you were sent here to heal it."

"Oh, Adam, no! I can't. Nobody could. It goes too deep. Katherine Trevinion is quite irrational in her prejudice, and the others follow her lead. I couldn't possibly make any impression on them."

"You can't say that until you've tried."

"I'm not the missionary type. I'm not tough enough," I pleaded. "How can I ever stand up to them? They'll try to possess me, to influence me, to bribe me into their way of thinking."

"Are you afraid that they may succeed?" His glance challenged me. "Afraid to put your faith to such a test?"

I shook my head confusedly. "It isn't quite that. It's more that I shall inevitably end up running from them as my mother did, and that'll leave my grandmother more hurt and bitter than ever. I would much rather spend the weekend here and— and not get any further involved with them."

He smiled then—that heartwarming, illuminating smile of his.

"There's nothing Aunt Araminta and I would like better than to keep you here," he said frankly, and his eyes told me that he wasn't referring just to the weekend. "Only, you're not your mother. You come from a totally different background. You haven't her excuse for flight, and they can't hurt you in the way they must have hurt her. Your armor hasn't been recently acquired; you've worn it all your life. Are you afraid to rely on it now?"

"You mean the sword of the Spirit and the helmet of

salvation? My grandmother doesn't recognize their existence. She'll hammer at me—" I lifted my chin. "No, I'm not afraid the armor will fail me. I'm just shirking the arguments and the unpleasantness. Because she is my mother's mother, she has me at a disadvantage."

"I understand," he said quietly, and I was convinced that he really did.

Then Miss Araminta came bustling from the kitchen, and I had to explain my position to her. She took it in her stride, and insisted on accompanying me upstairs to help me repack our suitcases.

"No need to distress yourself, my dear," she assured me briskly. "It's my belief that you were sent here—to us and to that unhappy household at the manor. Your arrival may well be the turning point—for Adam and for the Trevinions."

"I'm not likely to exert the least bit of influence on the Trevinions."

"I believe you can and will," she said firmly. "There's good material in that child, Kay, in spite of her wild, irresponsible behavior. Mrs. Trevinion will ruin her life and her brother's if someone doesn't intervene."

"I remember reading somewhere about the burden of an answered prayer. I didn't pray that I might get away from Kelchester, but often I longed to escape," I said impulsively. "I couldn't bear to leave Mother, but I wasn't really happy at home. I was always on the defensive with Father and his sister. Now I realize how fortunate I was to have been adopted by Father and Mother instead of by Katherine Trevinion."

"Then your trip down here is already bearing fruit," she said calmly. "Just 'trust in the LORD,' dear, and 'lean not unto thine own understanding.' It will all work out."

"How?" I asked desperately. "My grandmother says there's quite a lot of money for me from my mother's share of a trust fund. How can I make her see that I don't want it?"

"If it's yours, why refuse it? Take it and use it as your mother would have wished."

"*How?*" I asked again.

"You could begin by replacing the sadly tattered hymn-books in the church here. You could pay for electricity to be brought to the church and this part of the village. There are a hundred and one things crying out to be done," Miss Araminta said practically. "If old Mrs. Williams recovers from this second stroke, she'll need a wheelchair. The doctor says she can't hope to regain the use of her paralyzed leg. In spite of the welfare state, there are people here in genuine need. You can help them, and others."

"Yes, of course. I hadn't thought of that," I said in compunction. "People in Father's parish too. Aunt Clara has been organizing a fund in Kelchester to give hard-worked mothers with young children a holiday by the sea next summer. And there's an old people's home in which Mummie takes a keen interest—"

"You'll find plenty of outlets for your money, once you begin to look for them. Regard yourself as a steward, as your mother would have done," she advised me.

"I can try, but my grandmother won't see it that way. She'll reason that if I accept the money, I'll be under an obligation to the Trevinion family. She'll expect me to respect her wishes."

I couldn't tell her that Katherine had already proposed, quite seriously, that I should marry Seamus and settle down at the manor; presumably, in due course, to present her with great-grandchildren. Kindly, forthright Miss Araminta could have no idea of how autocratically and possessively Queen Katherine ruled her small kingdom. In this day and age, she was an anachronism clinging to a long-outdated feudal system. Had St. Petroc's been less isolated, it couldn't have worked. As it was, I had gathered from the Denvers that most of the young people rebelled and moved away as soon as they could.

James was showing signs of impatience—walking up and down on the mossy gravel and glancing repeatedly at his wristwatch—when I rejoined him. Adam brought our suitcases down to the car.

"Shall I see you tomorrow?" he asked. "In church?"

"Tomorrow? Oh, of course, it's Sunday tomorrow! I seem

145

to have lost count of time," I said confusedly. "Yes. I'll be there."

Adam only said: "Good!" but once again the look in his eyes was eloquent.

As we drove away, James said shortly: "You'll have to watch out for that fellow. A bit smitten, isn't he?"

"Do you think so?" I said demurely, hoping he wasn't aware of my quickened heartbeats.

"You're a very lovely girl, and now it seems that you're an heiress too," he answered significantly.

"Adam wouldn't take the Trevinion money into consideration," I said impulsively.

"Why not? A parson is a man like any other, and more in need of a wealthy wife than most."

I didn't answer. We drove over the narrow bridge in silence. James negotiated it with horn-blowing and his usual caution.

Presently, he said with satisfaction, "At any rate, if you stay on here, you'll have every excuse for not appearing in court."

"Oh!" I had virtually forgotten about that horrible court case. "I'll have to be back in Kelchester for that."

"It's not necessary," James said briefly. "The police have your statement."

"Yes, but it conflicted with Mike's. If I'm not there to answer questions, the judge may accept his version."

"What if they do? Do you want Mike O'Donnell to suffer for it?"

"No, but he shouldn't be allowed to get away with a bare-faced lie," I protested. "I don't dislike Mike, but I detest that 'money talks' attitude of the O'Donnells."

"My dear, that's the way the world spins. You can't alter it," James said philosophically.

James didn't want to alter it, I thought wryly. He was obviously impressed by the Trevinions and their money.

Lunch in a vast, oak-paneled dining room, its walls hung with oil paintings of past Trevinions, was quite a banquet. I could sense that James was admiring the heavy old silver, the cut glass and the delicate china. He liked what he would call "the good things of life." He ate heartily of the asparagus

146

soup, grilled trout, roast pheasant and Charlotte Russe. So did everyone else, except myself and Monica.

Dorothea was still asleep. Katherine said that it would be a pity to disturb her; she would ring for a tray to be taken up to her when she woke. It didn't apparently dawn on Katherine that Dorothea and I weren't in the habit of "ringing for trays" or of being waited on by an elderly butler and an immaculately spruce parlormaid.

I longed for Dorothea's support. Two kinds of wine were served, and I was the only person who refused them. Katherine eyed my glass of water disapprovingly.

"I hope you're not refusing this excellent Burgundy on principle, Lyra?" she said critically. "I've no patience with total abstinence. Educated people should know how much they can drink with safety."

Seamus quirked an eyebrow at me sardonically and Monica smiled bleakly. The twins were staring at me. James was looking embarrassed. They were all suddenly silent, waiting for my answer. I felt my cheeks burning.

"Father and Mother both abstain, so naturally Dorothea and I do too," I said with an effort. "Father follows St. Paul's teaching, 'If meat makes my brother to offend—' "

"Meat? What has meat to do with it? You're not a vegetarian," Katherine said impatiently.

"It's a quotation," I said awkwardly. "Father thinks we should set an example by avoiding anything which offends people."

"A strange kind of reasoning! You'll offend our friends if you ask for water at a party," Katherine said sharply. "I hope you're not a prig, child?"

"Oh, no! I've been called lots of things, but never that," I assured her. "I just happen to think that Father and Mother are right."

"Don't refer to those people as Father and Mother! You're a Trevinion. You must change your name to Trevinion, as the twins have changed theirs," Katherine said possessively.

"Thank you, but I wouldn't care to do that. Not even your

147

daughter Grace could have been a more wonderful mother to me than Anne Haughton has been," I said steadily.

"I warned you, Katherine," Seamus interposed with grim amusement. "This young woman is as stubborn as Grace was. If you push her too far, she'll walk out on us."

"Nonsense! She's my granddaughter," Katherine reminded him, but there was a faint uneasiness in her glance at me. As if to reassure herself, she added, "She'll soon get into our ways."

13

"THEA SHOULDN'T DREAM of attempting the long drive back to Kelchester tomorrow afternoon," James said with an unfamiliar air of decision. "I'll explain to your parents and they can contact the college. No need to alarm them by phoning."

Dorothea had managed to limp downstairs with my help that morning, but it had been obvious that she had found the effort painful. The long drive would be too hard on her, I agreed, but was she resigned to staying here? I glanced at her uncertainly.

"I suppose I can't very well get to the college until my ankle's better," she said doubtfully. "Only, I don't want to keep you here, Lyra, if you'd rather go home with James."

"I've promised to stay till after next weekend," I said reluctantly. "Apparently I have to see the Trevinions' lawyers, and there are things of my mother's which need to be sorted. Her room is exactly as she left it."

Katherine had shown me Grace's room last night. It had given me a shock to see the handsome, monogrammed brushes set out on the dressing table, and the rows of clothes, carefully preserved with mothballs.

"She took so little with her, my poor baby! That was why I was sure she would come home again," Katherine had said sadly. "She left all her lovely evening dresses, and her mink jacket and her riding clothes. The jewelry we gave her on her twenty-first birthday, too—an emerald and pearl necklace and bracelet, and a wristwatch to match. Can you understand it?"

"If my father was working in the East End of London, I suppose she thought such luxurious things would be inappropriate," I had answered, but I had guessed that Grace's reasons had gone deeper than that.

She must have felt a compulsion to free herself from the trappings of wealth. Perhaps she had hoped that by abandoning them she would convince her family that her heart was set on the "true riches." She might also have been anxious not to emphasize to my father that she had been brought up in a very different world from his.

"Well, they're yours now. You must go through them and decide what's worth keeping," Katherine had insisted. "It'll be a relief to Monica to have this room in use again. She has always fretted over "Grace's shrine," as she calls it. I'm afraid Monica is a very jealous woman, but she has to remember that she's not of my own blood."

"If you stay, I'll stay too," Dorothea said steadily.

"Splendid! I'll come down again next weekend and see how you're faring," James said briskly. "Take things easy and enjoy your taste of luxury."

"I won't enjoy it, but I don't want to leave Lyra at the Trevinions' mercy," Dorothea retorted in her forthright fashion.

"You absurd child!" James said tolerantly, and turned to me. "I gather that we're to be taken on a grand tour of the estate this morning."

"This morning?" I echoed in dismay. "What about church?"

"We do enough churchgoing in Kelchester. It won't hurt us to miss morning service once," James said cheerfully. "Wiser to humor your grandmother. She has it all arranged. Seamus is driving us around in his Land Rover."

I wondered uneasily if Katherine had planned the excursion in order to prevent me from going to church and, contacting the Denvers, I discovered later that this was the usual Sunday morning ritual. Monica was excused because she had "no present or future interest in the estate" as Katherine phrased it. Jay and Kay were compelled to accompany her on this weekly tour, during which Seamus was expected to give a full account of the past week's activities. So, I soon realized, were the Trevinions' tenants.

I sat beside her in the Land Rover. The twins gratefully rode in James' car. The countryside was beautiful and the farmlands, to my inexperienced eyes, looked well kept, but Katherine's running commentary made it impossible for me to relax. Her sharp eyes spotted the least flaw and she duly took the offender to task. A gate off its hinges, a fallen tree which hadn't been cleared away, a gap in a hedge through which sheep were getting out, piles of brambles which had been cut but not yet burned, a haystack which looked in imminent danger of collapsing, a crop of roots which was overgrown with charlock and spotted persicaria, two sacks of potatoes left by a field gate, and a garbage pail outside a farmhouse door were all noted by her, and severe reproofs administered.

I felt increasingly embarrassed every time we drew up at a farmhouse and Seamus summoned the farmer with imperative blasts on the horn. Seamus appeared to take Katherine's reprimands for granted, but I hated the chilly authority with which they were administered. She was treating these grown men as if they were naughty children.

Sometimes their wives came out with them, flushed and propitiatory. I almost expected them to curtsey. When Katherine introduced me, the look in their eyes made me writhe inwardly. I felt that they were automatically resenting me. The Trevinions might be feared, but they certainly weren't loved. I thought how different this tour would have been had Mummie been sitting beside Seamus. She would have listened sympathetically to the problems which some of the wives ventured to mention. She would have warmed them with her understanding. She would have asked about their families. Mummie really cared about people, but Katherine seemed to despise them.

As we were driving away from one small farmhouse where the farmer's wife, a young woman with a baby in her arms and a toddler clinging to her skirts, had pleaded for water to be piped into the farmhouse because she found carrying water from an old well burdensome, Katherine turned to me sharply.

"You're very quiet, Lyra. Beginning to realize the responsibilities of managing an estate as big as ours with tiresome people trying to exploit us all the time?" she challenged me. "Can't carry a bucket of water, indeed, at her age! Lazy thing!"

"I'm beginning to realize that the Trevinions don't believe in loving their neighbors," I was goaded into retorting. "How would you like to have to pump and carry water and heat it on an old range, with two young children's washing to tackle?"

"Don't talk nonsense! People like that are used to such conditions. They're brought up with them; just as we're used to good service," she said scathingly. "You can't compare a Mabel Penrose with the Trevinions."

"She's a human being too. Not a—a tractor. She's just as prone to deadly fatigue and backaches as a Trevinion."

"You silly child! If we once agreed to modernize any of these farmhouses, all the tenants would be badgering us," she said impatiently.

"And why not? In Kelchester such primitive conditions would never be tolerated."

"Loving one's neighbor can be pretty costly," Seamus interposed dryly, but there was something in his eyes which was like a spasm of pain. "Heavens, how often I used to argue that point with Grace! You're her daughter, sure enough."

"You failed to tame Grace because you were overconfident. See to it that you don't let her daughter elude you," Katherine said abruptly.

That caught me off guard. I glanced desperately at Seamus, hoping that he would laugh at this preposterous notion of hers. Instead, his face seemed to darken and his hard lips twisted.

"You don't have to apply any spurs," he said shortly, and it was Katherine who laughed.

It was an uncomfortable morning, and the conversation at

152

lunch did nothing to soothe my ruffled, exasperated feelings. Katherine was recalling what we had seen, and the warnings she had administered.

Suddenly she turned to me with "It's a fine estate, though, you'll agree, Lyra? Aren't you proud to know that it's ours?"

"Yours," I amended. "Yes, it could be a wonderful place."

"If you play your cards well, it could be yours," she hinted. "Worth making a few sacrifices for, isn't it?"

That was almost what Mike O'Donnell had said to me on another occasion, about all he had to offer me, I remembered with a pang. "All the kingdoms of this world *if*—" Neither he nor Katherine seemed to grasp the vital significance of that "*if*."

Everyone was looking at me speculatively as I hesitated. Katherine made an impatient little gesture.

"Well? Lost your tongue? Wouldn't you love to be mistress of such an inheritance?" she persisted.

"It would be a tremendous responsibility," I answered slowly. "To feel that the well-being of all those tenants was to some extent on one's shoulders would be a daunting prospect."

"Oh, nonsense! You took their requests much too seriously. If they're not satisfied with their conditions, they can always leave. There's no difficulty about getting new tenants, and at higher rents too," she said swiftly. "Didn't it give you a thrill to know that all you saw this morning belongs to the Trevinions? We count for something, child."

"Too much. All that land," I said confusedly. "The money and the power—"

"Dazzled?" Monica asked with her frosty smile.

"No. Overwhelmed," I answered candidly. " 'To whom much is given, of him shall much be required.' I wouldn't be a good enough steward."

"You wouldn't have to worry about the financial side; Seamus sees to that," Katherine said, staring at me in perplexity.

"I wasn't thinking of that. Those people—" I fumbled desperately for the right words. "One would have to care so much—give so much of oneself—if one were responsible for them. I suppose I'm not unselfish enough—not dedicated."

My voice trailed away because they were looking at me as if I were speaking a foreign language; all of them except Dorothea, who was nodding gravely. There was an uneasy pause.

"I know what Lyra means," Kay said abruptly, her color rising. "The Trevinions don't care; she does. And when I think about it, I find it's sickening too. The way we just exploit everyone, I mean."

"You either use people or else they use you," Jay drawled. "It's more profitable to wield the whip."

"Within reason. From what I saw, this estate is admirably run," James interposed pacifically. "It must be your personal supervision which keeps your tenants on their toes, Mrs. Trevinion. There's an oddly old-world atmosphere about this place."

"Like Dartmoor and the prison," Kay muttered rebelliously.

But Katherine ignored her and turned smilingly to James. "Yes. I'm sure the personal touch matters. My granddaughter may be afraid now that she couldn't cope, but it's just a question of training."

"Lyra tends to underestimate herself. She has brains. She did extremely well at school, and she's a highly competent secretary," James assured her. "You'll find her a more than adequate assistant here."

"She drives, of course? We must get her a car of her own."

Apparently James had restored her good humor. They fell to discussing what car would be most suitable for me. I could have anything I desired; the price didn't enter into it.

"I've so many birthday and Christmas presents to make up to my granddaughter," Katherine declared, and the look in her eyes smote me.

She obviously felt that she had been cruelly and unfairly deprived of her granddaughter. She resented the fact that my love and loyalty had been given to people who were not blood relatives; she wanted to feel that they were hers now. It was almost as though she were trying to bribe or force me to love and admire her.

I felt guilty of unkindness because I couldn't respond. Love didn't come to me easily. I had never really loved Father or Aunt Clara. I hadn't fitted in with them, and I could never fit in here. Perhaps I wasn't sufficiently tolerant or adaptable. Yet, I had instantly been at home with the Denvers.

When we were crossing the hall to the drawing room for coffee, Monica fell into step beside me, observing coldly, "You're privileged, Lyra. I hope you appreciate it."

"What do you mean?" I asked blankly.

"I've never been given a car of my own, but then I'm not one of the elect. A daughter-in-law doesn't rate in comparison with a granddaughter. I'm only a Trevinion by marriage," she said bitterly. "With you, it's a question of 'Ask, and it shall be given you.' A car, furs, jewels, money to burn, and even Seamus. Aren't you lucky?"

Her voice when she had said "Seamus" had been all too revealing. I looked at her in compassion which I dared not attempt to express.

"You don't understand," I said haltingly. "Those things aren't that important. I would like a car of my own, naturally, but—"

"Not at the price?" Her lips curved upward skeptically. "Aren't you for sale?"

"No, I'm not. As for Seamus, that's utterly preposterous."

"He doesn't think so. Haven't you noticed the gleam in his eyes when he looks at you? He plans to take his revenge on your mother through you," she said in a lowered tone. "That lawyer friend of yours doesn't stand a chance against the vaunted Trevinion determination. You have been warned!"

"Thank you, but the warning was unnecessary. James is merely a family friend," I said hastily. "More my sister's than mine."

James had his arm around Dorothea's waist and was helping her across the hall. Whether he realized it or not, he was more drawn to Dorothea than to me. I was too independent by nature for his taste; too ready to argue instead of accepting his masculine superiority.

"That's a pity," Monica said, as if to herself.

"Please," I said impulsively, "don't resent me. I haven't come here to usurp your position in any way. And nothing would induce me to—to give Seamus his revenge, as you put it."

"Nothing?"

"No. As a matter of fact, I'm in love already."

"At your age, and with your looks, romances come and go."

"Not with me. I've never been in love before; I never shall be again." I heard myself saying the words with a conviction which gave me a shock. Was I really sure I felt like that about Adam?

Yes, I was sure, because even to think of him was revitalizing. Only a few hours now before I saw him again. Nothing and no one could prevent me from going to the evening service.

Unfortunately Queen Katherine had other ideas for me. At teatime, she announced in her imperious fashion that I could get out Jay's sports car and drive her over to see some friends who had a "nice old place" six miles away.

"I want to introduce my lovely new granddaughter to them. I shall be interested too to see how you handle an Alfa Romeo," she added, smiling at me.

Jay muttered something sulkily and glowered at me. How typical to have bought such an expensive car for the boy and then to have taken it away from him! I thought ruefully. Miss Araminta was right. Katherine, with her mixture of arbitrary authority and overindulgence, was in danger of ruining the twins' characters.

"Some other time," I answered.

She said with gay derision, "Nervous? Then, I'll drive. I'm still young enough to enjoy handling a powerful car. You'll see!"

"I'm sorry, but this evening I'm going to church," I said quietly.

156

"Church? Didn't I tell you that the Trevinions had severed all connections with St. Petroc's?"

"I haven't. I promised the Denvers I would be there. At home, we usually attend two if not three services every Sunday."

"You're not in Kelchester now," Katherine said angrily. "I won't have you getting involved with those Denvers. I forbid you to go. Is that clear?"

"I'm sorry, but you can't do that," I said as evenly as I could. "I'm not a child; I have to make my own decisions about things like church attendance."

"Even though I'm your grandmother and you're a guest in my house?" she demanded. "Think well what you're doing, Lyra! I'm not accustomed to having my wishes disregarded."

"Lyra has been my parents' daughter for nearly twenty-three years. You can't expect her to abandon all they've taught her in one weekend here," Dorothea said indignantly.

"How true!" Monica commented bleakly. "It takes time both to form and to break habits. I used to go to church here when I was Lyra's age, until I realized that it was just a waste of time."

"Time—" Katherine echoed. With one of her swift, unpredictable changes of mood, she smiled at me. "Yes, I must give you time, child. I've always been impatient. Perhaps that was how I lost contact with your mother. Take your foster sister to church if she insists. The twins can come to Venrose Hall with me. I'll invite the Venroses over to meet you. We'll have a big dinner party."

In some ways, she was oddly childlike. She seized upon the idea of a dinner party and began to plan which friends she would invite. She appealed to the twins for suggestions, and accepted Jay's uncritically. She even teased him playfully about his girl friends. She was suddenly fond and indulgent toward him. It was as if she was trying to incite my jealousy, reminding me that I wasn't her only grandchild.

Jay responded eagerly. He had his grandmother's way of swinging rapidly from one mood to another, I perceived. Feeling himself restored to favor at my expense, he stopped

157

sulking and positively sparkled. Kay eyed him with a most unchildlike look of cynicism. She was the more adult and realistic of the pair, I thought. The stronger character too.

Seamus had taken James off for the afternoon, on Katherine's instructions. Seamus had some errand on a distant farm which Katherine had recently acquired, and she had virtually compelled James to go with him "while the girls have a rest," she had said. They returned just after we had finished tea. Katherine and the twins had gone upstairs to get ready for their excursion. The twins had been ordered to change from their slacks and jerseys into "respectable suits."

Monica ordered fresh tea for the two men and sat down again to play the hostess. James asked about our plans for the evening; then he firmly vetoed Dorothea's suggestion that he might drive us to church. It would be most unwise for Dorothea to impose such a strain on her ankle, he protested. Moreover, she would look dreadfully conspicuous, limping into church and remaining seated during the service.

That floored my poor young sister. Like James, she had a horror of being the least bit conspicuous. She was forced to agree to his alternative proposal that they should drop me at the church and then go for a short drive till the service was over.

"Don't bother about meeting me! I can easily walk back. I would like a walk," I said hastily. "I need to stretch my legs."

It was quite an effort to slow my steps to a decorous pace when they left me outside the church gate. I felt like some hunted animal heading for sanctuary, or a storm-tossed craft with a safe harbor within sight. So much had happened since we had left Kelchester. Mentally and emotionally, I was bruised and troubled. The small, weather-beaten old church seemed to stand for the only peace and certainty I knew. It had stood here for centuries. It would still be here, offering the same eternal promise and security, long after all the Trevinions of today had been forgotten.

After the sunshine outside, the interior of the church was dim. In my haste I didn't notice the three steps which led down

158

from the door. I stumbled and might have fallen, sprawling, but a wizened, elderly man grasped my arm and steadied me.

"Oh, thank you!" I said breathlessly.

"They steps is tricky. I allus waits here to give the old 'uns a hand down 'em," he explained with a friendly smile. Then he stepped back, staring at me. "Why, 'tis a Trevinion—a red-haired Trevinion—like our Miss Grace."

"Her daughter," I said with a current of warmth rushing through me. "You knew her?"

"For sure. I was verger here when she were christened, bless her! Her daughter, be you? The Lord be praised!" he said fervently. "'Twill be good to see Miss Grace's daughter a-sitting in that ole pew where she used to sit."

That gave me back the feeling I had had when we had first arrived in the village—a sense of continuity and of kinship with my mother. I smiled at him gratefully. He turned away to get a prayer and hymnbook for me, and I saw Adam. Tall and impressive in his black cassock, he was standing in a recess behind the font, tolling a bell. Our eyes met, and I saw his light up, as if he were unfeignedly glad to see me.

We didn't speak but, as I followed the old verger up the nave to the large, impressively carved oak pew of the Trevinions, I could almost feel the warm, strong clasp of Adam's hand on mine. That instant sense of recognition between us at our first encounter had been real and lasting, I thought thankfully. We had been meant to meet. We had, without knowing it, been waiting for each other. I might so easily have married James or Mike—as my mother might have married Seamus. Never, in my wildest dreams, had I visualized myself as a parson's wife. Nor, I guessed, had she. Yet she had been led to my father as I had been led to Adam.

I knelt on the worn hassock where perhaps my mother had once knelt, my heart so full that no coherent words would come to me. I tried to thank God for bringing me here—to pray for patience and wisdom and courage, that I might be shown how to cope with the Trevinions, that, somehow, I might ease Adam's struggle instead of adding to the Trevin-

159

ions' hostility against him. A sudden movement beside me brought me from my knees.

To my astonishment, Kay was endeavoring to slip in beside me.

"Move over, can't you?" she hissed.

I made room for her and she sat down, her chin tilted at a defiant angle, as if daring me to question her presence. She was looking older and unfamiliarly well groomed in a neat dark blue coat and skirt and a crisp white blouse, her long dark hair tied into a ponytail. I didn't speak and after a long moment she turned to me with a wry grin.

"Surprise?" she whispered. "Queen Katherine refused to take me to Venrose Hall unless I wore a hat. She knows I don't have any hats. It was just an excuse because she wanted Jay to herself. Anyway, I blew up, and then I thought I'd join you and risk being turned out by Adam Denver because I was bareheaded. Do you suppose he'll object?"

"I'm sure he won't. Even in Kelchester girls come to Father's church without hats," I whispered back.

"You're wearing one."

"I like hats; they keep down my unruly hair. I'm very glad you came, Kay."

Her lips quirked upward mischievously.

"Hoping that our brand-new vicar will convert me? He hasn't any use for me. He always keeps me at a discreet distance—for fear of Queen Katherine's wrath, I imagine. Or perhaps I shock him."

"Parsons, like doctors, aren't easily shocked."

I wished she wouldn't chatter. I wanted to sit quietly and absorb the atmosphere, but I hesitated to appear to snub her.

"Look!" she whispered, running a finger over some marks in the dark oak. "Grandfather carved his initials here when he was a small boy. So did his son—Aunt Monica's husband. Grandfather used to take his children to church when they were kids. Then there was some quarrel over the Glebe lands, and he became nearly as antichurch as Queen Katherine. The Trevinions can't bear to be crossed."

160

I nodded. Then the bell ceased to toll, and the elderly lady at the organ began, rather tremulously, to play. There were only a few daisies in the vases on the altar, I noticed. The church looked clean and well cared for, but everything was rather worn, like the shabby hymn and prayer books the verger had found for me. Were there no prosperous people among the parishioners who could afford to replace those books and the faded altar cloths? Were there no bell-ringers?

As we rose to sing the opening hymn, "Fight the Good Fight," I glanced over my shoulder. This was a small church but, even so, the congregation looked pitiably sparse. There were about twenty in all, I surmised, including Kay and me and Miss Araminta, the organist and the old verger. My heart ached for Adam as he walked slowly up the nave. He looked so young and so much alone; St. Petroc's didn't seem to have any choir.

Father had often said that a large congregation was an inspiration. He was a gifted preacher, but he admitted that he found it hard to do his best when he was asked to preach in a small country church. He was always most eloquent when he was preaching in the cathedral or at harvest festivals, when people turned out in force.

Why had Miss Araminta urged Adam to take this parish? Didn't she realize how discouraging it must inevitably be to a young, inexperienced but idealistic man? How could he hope to succeed where other vicars had failed? Most parsons had to fight a paralyzing apathy, but here Adam was up against active hostility. "Fight the good fight?" Oh, he would fight, because he was essentially a fighter, but what support could he hope for from this handful of middle-aged and elderly people? Kay and I must be the only two here, except for Adam himself, who were under forty.

I loved to sing. At home, of course, I was in the choir. Now, for the first time in years, I was self-conscious about my voice. It had so much volume that it sounded almost as if I were singing a solo until Adam reached the pulpit and began to sing too in a clear, pleasing tenor. Then it was more like a duet, with the other voices forming a ragged chorus.

I glanced down at Kay. She was staring fixedly at the words in the hymnbook. Her lips were curved in that unyouthful, cynical line, as if she found the words incredible. Then, with a slight shrug of her shoulders, she raised her chin and joined in the third verse.

Cast care aside, lean on thy Guide,
His boundless mercy will provide.

It would, too. Why was I worried about Adam or about myself? I wondered with a stab of self-reproach. Couldn't I trust the Guide who had led me here?

14

ADAM WAS FORTUNATE to have a strong voice, clear and beautifully modulated. He read the prayers as if every phrase were full of meaning for him.

He took his sermon from the text, "Put on the whole armour of God . . . above all, taking the shield of faith."

I wondered if it were a coincidence or if he had been thinking of me when he had chosen that theme. His preaching was characteristic of him—direct, simple and utterly sincere. He didn't have Father's scholarly approach or well-measured, polished phrases, but he had a kind of fervor which was more compelling than any eloquence. Even Kay seemed impressed by it. She had been restless during the prayers and Scripture reading. Now she was motionless, her eyes fixed on Adam, her forehead creased, as if she were listening to words in a foreign language.

Perhaps "only believe and thou shalt see" was foreign to her generation, which attached so much importance to proof. Perhaps Kay herself hadn't much reason to trust anyone, I thought compassionately. Seamus showed her a certain careless indulgence, but Monica had plainly no use for her, and Katherine obviously favored her brother. Perhaps Kay had never known the affection and security which every child should have. Certainly she hadn't been taught to "put on the

163

whole armour." She was restless and frustrated and rebellious. I found myself praying desperately that something of what Adam was saying might touch her heart.

When we rose to sing the closing hymn, "At even, ere the sun was set," Kay still wore that thoughtful, abstracted expression. After the benediction, she knelt, motionless, for a minute or two.

Then, rising, she said hurriedly, "Come on! Let's go."

I would have liked to linger and say good night to Adam, but he was standing on the porch, talking to a big bearded man. Kay caught my arm and tugged me impatiently past them. Outside, the light was fading fast and I couldn't see her face clearly. I heard her draw a quick, deep breath.

Then she said jerkily, "He's really sold on all that, isn't he? It isn't just a job to him."

"No. It's a great deal more," I said hesitantly.

" 'Thy touch has still its ancient power,' " she quoted. "You believe that, don't you, Lyra?"

"Yes."

"Then, you won't think I'm crazy—" She paused, then went on in a rush. "When he was saying 'the peace of God which passeth all understanding,' I had the strangest sensation. As if there was a touch—a hand on my head—and a kind of peace surging into me. *Peace!* That's something I've never had before and never wanted, at least not consciously, though sometimes I have shrunk from all the bickering and discord in the house."

She had stopped halfway to the gate, as if to let the rest of the congregation disperse ahead of us. She was running one hand over the worn gray stone of the wall.

She added, on a note of appeal, "It's true, isn't it? 'Only believe.' If I had 'the shield of faith,' I wouldn't be stung by Aunt Monica and Queen Katherine's darts into doing stupid things. I wouldn't let them laugh me out of the one thing I really want."

"To be a nurse?"

"Yes. That last hymn made me realize it. We often sang that hymn at my first school when I was a child. I had a vivid, mental picture of Christ, with all those sick people gathering round Him. I used to think how wonderful it must have been to have that power to heal." She drew a deep breath. "Just now, it came home to me what a sick and sorry mess I'd made of myself and how much I needed that healing before I could hope to heal anyone else. Then it seemed like an answer to a prayer I hadn't consciously prayed. Was it imagination, do you suppose, or was it true?"

"I'm quite sure it was real," I answered thankfully. "That's how God works. Someone sent Mummie some verses she loves, called 'Blessing Unknown.'

> Call and the Lord will answer;
> Even before your cry,
> He will have made provision,
> Help will be drawing nigh.

"That's true, Kay. I've proved it."

She nodded slowly and turned toward the gate.

" 'Only believe,' " she said again, after a pause. "I'm certainly going to need that shield Adam talked about when Queen Katherine knows. Seamus will laugh in that derisive way of his; and Jay takes his cue from Seamus. I hate being laughed at, Lyra. Don't you?"

"Not more than most of us. Sometimes, I'm afraid I don't care enough what people think of me," I said candidly. "As Seamus says, there's an awful stubborn streak in me."

"You're lucky. You're naturally lovely, and that always helps. You've a glorious voice too. Haven't you ever thought of being a professional singer?"

"Often. It was the career I wanted, but Father wouldn't agree."

If I had been a professional singer, I would never have come here, never have met the Trevinions or Adam, I realized suddenly. I could be glad now that Father hadn't listened to my pleas.

I heard firm, swift footsteps on the worn stone behind us. I didn't need to turn my head to know that they were Adam's.

165

The leap of my pulses was a sure indication. I should have guessed that he wouldn't let me go without a word.

"Lyra—Miss Trevinion," he called.

"Hello!" Kay said on a defensive note.

"It's getting dark. I'll see you as far as the lodge gates," he said, indicating the large flashlight he was carrying.

"Very chivalrous of you but there's no need," Kay responded with a wry grin. "It'll merely make our revered grandmother madder than ever if she learns that you walked us home. And Aunt Monica will make snide remarks about our reason for going to church."

"Your aunt was sitting with Mrs. Williams while Jim and his wife were at church. The old lady is making a wonderful recovery."

"Oh, good!" I said warmly.

So Monica did have kindly impulses. Perhaps hers was one of those unfortunate natures which had a secret yearning for friendship and affection, and yet by an astringent manner rebuffed people who would have offered them.

"You must look in on her, Lyra. She's longing to see Miss Grace's daughter, so Jim was telling me. She says that another red-haired Trevinion means the turn of the tide. The villagers attach great important to those old legends," Adam said reflectively. "The Williamses remember your father too. Jim was observing that you've inherited your father's voice."

That startled me. I hadn't guessed that my voice had come to me from my father. I had taken it for granted that Grace Trevinion had been the musical one.

"Apparently your father had the chance to become the equivalent of a modern "pop" singer in his teens, but he felt himself called to the ministry," Adam added. "He seems to have been a most inspiring preacher."

"You don't do so badly," Kay said with a kind of deliberate lightness. "You hit straight from the shoulder."

Before Adam could respond, the still night air was shattered by a horrible crashing sound. I recognized it instantly and in horror. It was the same tearing of metal, intensified, which I had heard when Mike had crashed his sports car.

166

"Someone's hit the bridge," Adam said, and broke into a run.

Kay and I were hard on his heels as he rounded the bend which led to that high, narrow old bridge. A large red car, its headlights still blazing, was upended like a child's discarded toy, its front wheels resting half over the stone parapet.

Beside me, Kay drew a sobbing breath.

"The Alfa! It's Jay's Alfa," she gasped. "Jay—oh, *Jay*—"

The beam of Adam's flashlight picked out the slight, crumpled figure lying just clear of the car, against the other side of the bridge. Kay seemed to fly past me to hurl herself to her knees beside that motionless figure.

"Careful! Don't try to move him," Adam said urgently, as she would have gathered her twin into her arms. "Let's see first if there are any broken bones."

"He's dead!" she screamed, staring with dilated eyes at that white, unconscious face so like her own. "He must have struck his head against the stonework."

Adam was kneeling beside her, opening Jay's shirt and feeling for his heart.

"No, he isn't dead, but I'm afraid he's badly hurt," he said quietly. "Run into the lodge and phone the doctor and an ambulance."

"You go, Lyra. I can't leave him," Kay said huskily.

"Right, but—but—Katherine," I faltered. "She was in the car with him. Where's Katherine?"

Adam stood up and directed his flashlight beam into the car. Katherine was crumpled behind the steering wheel, lying sideways half across the passenger seat. One arm was twisted under her at an unnatural angle and I guessed that it was broken. She looked dreadfully like a discarded doll, but she blinked as the light shone on her face, moved feebly, and groaned.

"Heavens! What's happened? I heard the crash as I was leaving the Williams' cottage—"

For once it was a relief to hear Monica's cool, crisp voice. She loomed up behind me and glanced over my shoulder.

"Looks as if they've had it," she observed unemotionally.

167

"Queen Katherine has been asking for it; she's as reckless a driver as Jay, and that's saying a lot. This bridge should have been widened years ago but she and Seamus wouldn't have it touched. An ancient landmark, they called it. Poetic justice that she should crash on it—"

"Would you go to the lodge, Mrs. Trevinion, and phone for the doctor and an ambulance?" Adam interposed swiftly. "Both your mother-in-law and Jay are in urgent need of medical attention."

"If they're not beyond it," Monica said cooly. "Oh, well, there won't be many tears shed for Queen Katherine! Yes, I'll go."

She stepped back and I heard the click of her heels as she walked on at a steady, unhurried pace.

"She doesn't care. She's utterly heartless," Kay's voice rose raggedly. "Oh, *Jay—*"

"Don't misjudge your aunt. Shock does strange things to people sometimes," Adam said evenly. "I think we'd better try to ease your grandmother out of the car, Lyra. It's in a precarious position. Can you reach her? I don't dare put my weight on it."

The door appeared to be jammed, but I managed to reach over it and get a grip of Katherine's shoulders. She groaned again and opened her eyes.

"Lyra? This is your fault," she said feebly. "I was coming to meet you, to stop you from fraternizing with those Denvers. I was afraid I would miss you; I took the bridge too fast."

"Don't worry about that now," I said hurriedly. "We must get you clear of the car in case it slips sideways. If you can slide your legs around, we can lift you out. Give me your hand."

I had to admire her fortitude. She must have been in great pain from that helplessly dangling right arm, but she didn't faint. She dragged herself clear of the steering wheel and, between us, Adam and I managed to lift her over the door.

"What about the boy? Is he all right?" she demanded as we lowered her gently to the ground.

168

"He was thrown clear; he's unconscious," Adam said briefly. "Your daughter-in-law has gone for help."

"I know. I heard her. Hoped I was dead, didn't she?" Katherine snapped. "I'm tougher than she guesses."

"Don't talk! Just lean against me and keep quiet till the doctor gets here," I said, dropping down beside her. "You've hurt your arm."

"Are you telling me what to do, child? If you hadn't been so stubborn, this wouldn't have happened," she retorted spiritedly. "If Jay's badly hurt, you'll be to blame."

"That's ridiculous, Mrs. Trevinion!" Adam said firmly. "You must have taken the bridge too fast."

Her uninjured hand was gripping my arm tightly and she was white to the lips, but she said fiercely, "Keep out of this, young man! And don't imagine that I shall let history repeat itself with my daughter's daughter. If you dare to look at her, I'll make this parish too hot to hold you."

He didn't answer except by a tautening of his fine figure. He turned away and knelt down beside Kay and her unconscious twin. Kay grabbed at his arm.

"*Pray!*" she said, in a shaken, tear-choked voice. "You believe. Let's see if your faith works. Pray for my brother. And you, too, Lyra. 'Call and the Lord will answer,' you said. Go on, then! *Call—*"

I felt a tremor run through Katherine's slight frame, but she didn't say anything. Perhaps she was realizing that this was a crisis in which all her determination, all the Trevinion money, and all their prestige were powerless to save Jay.

In his clear, unhurried voice, Adam began, "O Lord, help us—"

* * *

"Well?" Katherine demanded imperiously. "What's the news? Nobody here will tell me anything. I'm treated as if I were a newborn baby. I've told the doctor that I insist on being taken home tomorrow."

"You're certainly looking better," I said tentatively.

"Better? I'm not ill. A broken arm is an injury not an

169

illness," she said impatiently. "Don't try to humor me! I want the facts. How's the boy?"

"He's alive but not conscious yet," I answered, judging from her heightened color that to attempt to evade her questions would do her more harm than good. "His spine was injured when he was flung against the parapet. His skull too."

"It's a miracle that he's alive," Kay said in a strained voice from the chair on the other side of the hospital bed. "You nearly killed him and yourself. I don't know how to forgive you, but Lyra says I must. She made me come with her—"

"Nonsense! Accidents can happen to the best of drivers," Katherine retorted, turning her head to glower at Kay. "Forgive me, indeed! Things have come to a pretty pass if I'm to ask for forgiveness from a young girl like you."

"That accident wouldn't have happened if you hadn't been furious because Lyra had thwarted you by insisting on going to church," Kay said, gazing back at her unflinchingly. "I suppose you were showing off before Jay, too, trying to prove that you could handle that car better than he did!"

"Don't be impertinent, child!"

"You always think that anyone who dares to tell you the truth is being rude or impertinent," Kay said with a tilt of her chin. "You never gave Jay or me a chance to be ourselves. You treated us as if we were lapdogs, and we had to take it because we didn't have any money. You expected us to be grateful to you and do everything you said."

"That's enough! You're forgetting yourself," Katherine said sharply. "Where would you and your brother be now if I hadn't adopted you?"

"We might have been adopted by people like Lyra and Dorothea's parents. And—and Jay wouldn't be barely alive." Kay swallowed hard, then went on steadily, "I just want to make you understand, that's all."

"Understand what?" Katherine demanded.

"That I believe Jay would have died if it hadn't been for Lyra and Adam Denver's prayers. The doctor said it was a miracle which saved him. You taught us to scoff at miracles

170

and any kind of faith. Now it's only through a miracle that you didn't kill your grandson."

"Faith has nothing to do with it. If that young parson has been getting at you girls, he shall pay dearly for it," Katherine said angrily. "Taking advantage of my being laid up here, is he?"

"Adam doesn't enter into it. At least, not in the way you're implying," I interposed. "Kay is only trying to tell you that she believes our prayers were answered."

"And, when Jay is better, I'm going into nurse's training," Kay said steadily. "I want to help to heal people instead of plaguing them. You and Seamus incited us into tormenting everyone who opposed you. I'm ashamed now when I remember how we frightened that last vicar's wife into a nervous breakdown."

"Let's not go into that now," I said hurriedly, disturbed by Katherine's hectic color and quickened breathing.

Kay had told me about the tricks she and Jay had played. They had dressed up as ghosts and "haunted" the churchyard. They had hidden in the disused rooms of the old vicarage and made eerie noises when the vicar's wife had been alone there. They had blown out candles and turned out lamps whenever they could do so unobserved. They had crept into the vicar's study and disarranged his papers. Egged on by Seamus, their fertile imaginations had conceived many small ways of causing alarm and irritation, like the raids on Jim Williams' crab pots and long lines.

"I'm sorry. I just wanted you to understand," Kay said quickly. "I'm going to sit with Jay now."

Katherine didn't attempt to detain her. She was lying back against a pile of pillows, her uninjured hand clawing at the bedclothes, her lips twitching. As the door closed behind Kay, she gave me a piercing, challenging look.

"What's got into that child? Is this your doing, Lyra?" she demanded.

I shook my head. "Kay has just realized that 'underneath are the everlasting arms.' Try to be glad for her, Grandmother. She couldn't have borne this anxiety about her twin in her own strength," I said gently.

"Then, she's a weakling and no true Trevinion. I've never needed any strength except my own," she said firmly. "Kay always exaggerates. No need to work herself up about the boy; he's young and strong."

I hesitated to tell her just how serious Jay's injuries were, but it seemed that Kay had said enough to make Katherine insist on being given the facts.

When she was brought home two days later, my first thought was that Katherine had aged ten years. Her features seemed to have sharpened, her eyes looked sunken under her fine brows, and there were streaks of gray showing up in her dyed hair. A nurse came from the hospital with her and wanted to put her right to bed, but Katherine refused point-blank to be babied anymore.

When I was summoned to her room, I found her in an armchair beside a blazing fire, with a tea tray on a table beside her.

"You can pour tea for me," she greeted me abruptly. "I can't stand your aunt's chilly, grudging service. Monica hates and resents me. Do you realize that?"

"Have you ever loved her? Ever treated her as a daughter?" I countered. "You can command service, but you can't command affection, Grandmother."

"Nobody but you has ever dared to call me Grandmother. I tried to stay young—to be a companion to Seamus and Monica and the twins, but none of them really wanted me. All they cared about was what they could get out of me," she said bitterly. "I forced them to obey me, but I've had no real comfort from any of them. They've taken all I've given them. How much have they given me?"

"Perhaps you didn't show them that you cared about them. Perhaps you weren't generous in the right way," I said tentatively. "Money and power and pride are cold comfort."

"You're like your mother. She used to throw her arms around me and hug me when she was a child. But I was never demonstrative. I used to rebuff her—tell her not to be sentimental and soft." She sipped her tea with a faraway look in her eyes. Then she gazed at me challengingly. "I did my best for my family. I've worked and fought and planned to make the estate prosper. Now, who is to look after it when I've gone? I'm told that my only grandson will be a helpless cripple for the rest of his life."

"Not helpless. At least, not if the operation's successful," I said quickly. "He'll be able to get about again. He just won't be able to do anything strenuous."

"And they all blame *me* for it—Kay and Monica and Seamus. I suppose you'll say it's my fault too and not yours. Be honest with me, child! Am I to carry that burden to my dying day?"

"You don't have to carry it, Grandmother. It was your proud, unyielding, stubborn spirit which laid it on your shoulders," I said, trying desperately to find the right words. "You can be like Christian in *The Pilgrim's Progress*. You can let it roll off you where he did."

"Where was that? I haven't read the old fairy tale since I was a child."

"At the foot of the cross. 'Casting all your care upon him, for he careth for you.' That's the only way you'll ever find release—"

She checked me with an impatient gesture.

"Are you trying to convert me, child? At my age? What a hope!"

"It's never too late, Grandmother. Honestly and truly, there is no other way."

"That's what you've been taught to believe," she said scornfully. "To me, it's meaningless gabble."

Words were powerless to reach that proud, self-contained heart, I realized regretfully. She wouldn't listen to me or to Kay or to Dorothea. We could only pray for her. I knew Mummie would be praying too. I had written, telling her all about the Trevinions and about the accident. Her answering letter had been characteristic of her loving, unselfish spirit. Although she missed me very much, she felt that I was needed at the manor, and that Grace Trevinion would have wished me to help her mother through this time of anxiety. As for the trust fund I had mentioned, she said that she and Father would have to leave it to me to decide whether I accepted any part of it or not. They knew me well enough to be sure that it wouldn't influence my relations with the Trevinions in any way.

Father was concerned that Dorothea would miss more of the term at the college, so he had asked James to arrange to bring her home next weekend, Mother had added.

I was reluctant to lose Dorothea's staunch support. She was nearer in age to Kay than I was, and a genuine friendship had sprung up between them. Dorothea had her future career to consider though, and I couldn't hang onto her. The Trevinions were my affair rather than hers, and I had to cope with them as well as I could.

Both Adam and Miss Araminta had called to see Katherine, but she had refused ungraciously to see either of them. She had even forbidden me to ask them into the house and offer them tea. She had made unkind remarks about penniless young parsons and attractive heiresses, and it had been difficult for me to keep my self-control.

I was dreading the weekend. I didn't guess the surprise it held in store for me. We were expecting James to turn up on Saturday afternoon, spend the night at the inn, and drive Dorothea home the next day. It came as a profound shock when he arrived accompanied by Mike O'Donnell. I was too taken aback for words when Mike, as handsome, debonair and assured as ever, strode into the drawing room with James.

"Couldn't pass up this chance of seeing you, my love," Mike grinned and, before I could forestall him, he had flung his arms around me and kissed me. "How are you, my darling?"

We were all assembled in the drawing room for tea. I wrenched away from him, acutely conscious of Kay's wide-eyed stare, of Monica's raised eyebrows, and of Dorothea's startled gasp. Only Katherine appeared to take the demonstration in her stride.

"I felt sure that my lovely granddaughter must have some

romantic interest in her life," she observed, smiling approvingly at Mike. "Introduce us, child!"

Desperately embarrassed, I murmured a hurried introduction. Mike promptly seated himself beside Katherine and proceeded to turn his celebrated charm on her. She responded as I might have guessed she would. Mike was just the type to whom she would be drawn—poised, self-assured and obviously wealthy. He was the kind of husband she had picked out for her daughters; it was inevitable that she should approve of him as a suitor for her granddaughter.

I was cornered. I couldn't, with such an audience, tell Mike just what I thought of him and his audacity. I just had to seethe inwardly. It seemed incredible to me now that I could ever have been flattered by his attentions or agreed to think over his proposal.

He had his good points, of course. James had evidently told him all about the Trevinions on the drive down. Mike's solicitude seemed as genuine as James' and much more eloquently expressed, when he inquired about Jay, and sympathized with Katherine over her broken arm. He even asked kindly about Dorothea's ankle, and began to draw out Kay and Dorothea. He certainly had a way with him, but I longed to tell him that he was wasting his time. He might succeed in ingratiating himself with my family, but not all his charm could touch my heart.

Katherine, graciously seconded by Monica, invited both men to dine with us. When they had departed to deposit their luggage at the inn and change for dinner, she seemed to have regained something of her old fire and sparkle.

She turned to me and said gaily, "Well, that was a pleasant surprise! You've better taste than I had guessed, Lyra. Your Mike is a most attractive young man."

"Most of the girls in Kelchester would agree with you," I said quietly. "He's very popular. But he isn't *my* Mike."

"He intends to be; that's quite clear," she smiled. "I must confess that I'm relieved. In spite of your protests, I was afraid you might have a weakness for that estimable but unexciting young lawyer. James wouldn't be man enough for a spirited girl like you."

"Neither is Mike. He's too much the overindulged only son of wealthy and adoring parents. I suppose some girl will make a man of him some day, but I won't be that girl," I assured her.

"There's plenty of time! I'm not ready to hand my grand-daughter over to any man, however eligible, just yet," she said calmly. "He'll have to agree to a long engagement."

"Don't! Please listen to me. I became involved with Mike just by chance."

I began to explain about the accident, but she cut me short imperiously.

"I heard all that last weekend from James Mallard. İt was my suggestion that he should bring the young man down here with him," she said to my astonishment. "From what James told me, Mike O'Donnell sounded like just the man for you. I didn't mean for you to lose touch with him. I guessed that he might find counter attractions in Kelchester while you were off the scene."

"Oh, Grandmother!" I checked a sigh of exasperation. "Don't try to plan my life for me. You'll only be disappointed."

She wouldn't listen; she was plainly congratulating herself on her successful maneuver.

"It doesn't do to play too hard to get. You've already risked losing that young man by your stiff-necked attitude toward his accident. He must be really fond of you to have overlooked that," she admonished me. "Don't try his patience too far."

My heart sank. I had hoped that I had been getting closer to Katherine since she had come home from the hospital. But now it looked as if our viewpoints were as diametrically opposed as ever. She thought I should have backed up Mike's version of the accident, that I had been downright stupid to risk antagonizing him.

It seemed an interminably long evening. I managed to elude Mike's determined attempts to get me alone, but I realized that I couldn't put him off indefinitely. James warned me not to try.

"Mike's not going back to Kelchester before you've given him his answer," he told me. "He's completely sold on you, my dear. You can twist him around your little finger."

"For how long? It's no use, James," I said desperately. "Can't you make Mike see it?"

"Now, don't be silly!" James said in an older-brother fashion. "What do you have against Mike? He may have run wild in the past, but he's all set to settle down now. Don't forget that your circumstances have changed. As an heiress, you'll be a target for fortune hunters. Mike isn't in that category. He fell in love with you before he knew anything about the Trevinions."

I nearly said, "So did Adam Denver," but I had no grounds for such a statement.

That drawing together I had sensed between Adam and me might not, after all, be mutual. Adam had never said a word to indicate that he loved me. It might be that he saw my connection with the Trevinions as an insurmountable barrier.

I spent a restless, dream-haunted night. I woke early to a beautiful, sunny autumn morning. I almost wished that rain was lashing against the windows. It would have been more in tune with my mood. I felt disturbed and restless, as if I were being relentlessly driven by pressures which were increasingly difficult to resist. I wondered if my mother had felt the same way when Katherine had been working to throw her into Seamus' arms.

I got up quietly, so as not to wake Dorothea. I washed and dressed, and tiptoed from the bedroom. I could almost feel that Grace Trevinion was walking beside me as I let myself out of the house and headed for the path through the woods. I sensed intuitively that I was following in her footsteps, seeking the same refuge she had found.

177

15

THERE WERE ONLY half a dozen people gathered in the old church for the eight o'clock service. I couldn't bring myself to sit alone in the Trevinion pew, so I slipped into a seat beside Miss Araminta. She welcomed me with a smile which warmed my heart and took away that unnerving sensation of isolation.

Gradually, as Adam's clear voice read the familiar scriptures, peace seeped into me. So often in Kelchester and at the manor I had had an uncomfortable feeling that I didn't really belong, but in church I always had a sense of homecoming. In church I knew without any shadow of doubt that the eternal God was my refuge and underneath were the everlasting arms.

"Only believe." Nothing else mattered; of that I was utterly certain. I had to try to run the straight race with no wavering, whatever the cost to myself or to other people. I didn't want to hurt Katherine. I didn't want her to turn against me as she had turned against her own daughter, but I couldn't pay the price she was trying to exact from me for remaining in her favor. I had to hold fast to all that I believed. Perhaps I was stubborn by nature but, for me, there could never be any question of compromise.

When I knelt beside Miss Araminta at the altar rail and

178

heard Adam say those wonderful, familiar words, "Preserve thy body and soul into everlasting life," I seemed to feel new strength and vitality flowing into me.

Later, as we were heading for the porch, Miss Araminta laid a hand on my arm.

"Come and have breakfast with us, my dear. Jim brought us some freshly caught mackerel last night," she said hospitably.

I hesitated and she added, "Please! It would cheer Adam up to have a talk with you. You turned him away from the manor rather unceremoniously."

"That wasn't my doing. My grandmother flatly refused to let me ask him into the house," I said hurriedly.

"Then come with me now. We're eager to hear all your news," she said persuasively.

"Thank you! I would like to come."

"Good!" Still holding my arm, she steered me in the direction of the vicarage. "I've never had any patience with the pride that leads to misunderstandings."

Not knowing exactly what she meant by that, I glanced at her inquiringly.

"We saw Mr. Mallard on his way to the inn yesterday evening, and the friend who was with him," she said meaningfully. "It wasn't difficult to guess why they were down here."

"Mike O'Donnell isn't exactly a friend of James Mallard's. Mike's father happens to be one of the Mallards' most influential clients," I said hurriedly. "It was my grandmother who suggested that he should come down with James to take Dorothea home."

"Your grandmother's suggestion? Does she know the young man, then?" Miss Araminta asked in perplexity.

"No, but James had told her about him and she approved of what she'd heard. Even after the shock of the accident, she can't stop trying to manage her family's lives," I said ruefully. "She's just as stubborn as she says I am."

"Tell me about it," Miss Araminta said briskly. "It often helps to talk things over with a friend."

By the time the mackerel were sizzling in the frying pan, I had told her the whole story of my involvement with Mike.

She listened sympathetically, but she was smiling when I finished.

"My dear, I've misjudged you. I thought that you were badly worried when you came into church. I was all set to talk to you like a mother, but you don't need any advice from me. You've already made up your mind, haven't you?" she said.

"Yes," I answered, realizing that it was true. "Mike is a lot better than his reputation. He has definite potentialities. Only, not for me; never for me."

"Then you must brace yourself to make that quite clear to him," she said decisively. "You shrink from hurting people, I can see, but to be frank with them is more merciful in the end."

"I suppose so."

"Oh, yes! Don't make the mistake your mother did. She hurt her parents more by slipping away secretly than if she had faced them and told them straight out that she was determined to marry your father. The suspense in which she left them must have been hard for them to endure. It heightened your grandmother's bitterness because she blamed your father for it."

"Yes, I realize that. She still can't understand why my mother acted as she did and never wrote to tell her of my birth," I said slowly. "Perhaps I ought to show her my mother's letter to me."

"She hasn't read it?"

"No, I was afraid it would hurt her too much."

"Katherine Trevinion would prefer pain to bewilderment," Miss Araminta said with conviction. "A clean, sharp stab may be the only cure for the festering wound of resentment which the years have failed to heal."

I nodded. Then I felt my pulses quicken as I heard Adam's footsteps. He came striding into the kitchen, and his whole face seemed to light up as his glance met mine.

"Lyra! It's good to see you here again," he said, and took both my hands in his.

That firm, warm handclasp swept away all my misgivings. I

180

hadn't let my imagination run away with me; I didn't need any words to convince me that we belonged together.

I could never recall afterward what we spoke of as we ate the delicious fresh mackerel. Miss Araminta talked in her usual brisk, friendly way and I must have responded automatically. Just to be here with her and Adam was like being in a dream from which I dreaded to awaken. But after I had drunk a second cup of coffee and helped Miss Araminta wash the dishes, I had no excuse for lingering.

"I'll have to go now," I said regretfully. "My grandmother insisted last night that she was well enough for her customary Sunday morning tour of the estate, and she invited James and Mike to accompany us."

Adam's brows met as he walked with me to the door.

"Mike?" he echoed inquiringly.

"Your aunt will tell you about him if you want to know," I said hurriedly. "He isn't important."

"No?" He fell into step beside me as I turned down the moss-grown drive. "Just a friend?"

"Not even that."

We walked in silence for a moment or two.

Then he asked jerkily, "When shall I see you again?"

"Tonight, at the evening service."

"Good!"

There was another silence. I glanced up at him. It was as though there was suddenly an intangible barrier between us. Remembering what Miss Araminta had said about pride, I swallowed hard. Then I blurted out impulsively, "Any time you want me, Adam, you know where to find me."

"Any time?" he echoed. "It's all the time, Lyra. I suppose I haven't any right to tell you so—I've little enough to offer you—but I love you. I'll always love you."

"Oh, Adam! It's like that for me too."

I was in his arms, clinging to him, raising my lips to the firm yet tender pressure of his. I could feel his heart beating in time with my own. Joy surged all through me.

Then, with obvious reluctance, he released me.

"You're sure?" he asked with concern. "You do realize

181

what view the Trevinions will take of this? Your grandmother will never willingly let you marry me."

"She can't stop me. I was never more sure of anything, Adam," I answered steadily. "This is where I belong—with you, sharing your life."

"It'll be tough going. Perhaps you don't realize how tough. People will make unkind remarks about your money, and my lack of it."

"It isn't *my* money. I don't want it; we'll just use it as my parents would have done," I said swiftly. "It won't be any burden then. Don't worry! With you, I can face anything, however tough."

"Bless you, my darling! I believe you really mean that."

"Of course I mean it. I'll tell my grandmother as soon as I can get her alone. And I'll write to Mummie. Dorothea can take my letter back with her," I said resolutely. "Mummie will understand and be glad for me."

"Your grandmother will be furious. She'll feel that she has found you only to lose you again, as she lost your mother."

"She doesn't have to lose me. That's up to her."

"Would you rather I broke the news to her?"

I shook my head. "No, there's just a chance that I may be able to make her understand. I'll try not to hurt her in the way my mother did.

* * *

James was anxious to get back to Kelchester before dark. Mike told him teasingly that he was a regular old maid in his exaggerated caution and dislike of night driving, but James retorted tritely that he would always rather be safe than sorry. Besides, Dorothea would be returning to college tomorrow morning, so she should have an early night. Dorothea backed him up, so they left immediately after lunch.

I had the inevitable few minutes alone with Mike first, while Dorothea was getting ready. He marched me out onto the terrace with a proprietorial air. I could feel the significant glances of the Trevinions following us. So, it seemed, could Mike.

182

"I think I've scored a hit with your formidable relatives," he observed with obvious gratification. "Your grandmother told me that she had hoped you would settle for Cousin Seamus, but she had to admit that he was a long way removed from your age group. She's willing to concede that I'm a more suitable match for her lovely granddaughter. Are you ready to let me announce our engagement, my sweet?"

"I'm sorry, but the answer is no, Mike."

"Not yet? Why not?" he demanded.

"Not now—or ever. I'm already engaged to the man I love."

"What?" He looked as if I had struck him. "You can't be serious."

"I am. Completely."

"You'll take on that old sobersides Mallard? Oh, no! He would bore you stiff within a week. And you would drive him to distraction," Mike said incredulously.

"It isn't James."

"Who then? Surely not 'that impertinent, ubiquitous young parson' as your grandmother calls him? Are you crazy?"

"No, just very happy."

It wasn't easy to convince him that I was in earnest, but he realized it at last. He took it better than I might have expected.

"Well, you've certainly the courage of your convictions," he conceded. "You're letting yourself in for some stormy weather, you know. The Trevinions will write you off as a dead loss."

"I know. I'm prepared for rough going."

"Then all I can do is to wish you luck. You'll need it," he said grimly.

James was sounding his horn impatiently. We walked around the house to find Dorothea and James waiting in the car. Dorothea was in the back. I opened the door to kiss her good-bye, and she flung her arms around me and hugged me.

"Take care of yourself, Lyra. I hate having to leave you," she said unsteadily.

"I wish you didn't have to go. It's been a great comfort to

have you here." I kissed her warmly, then whispered, "Be nice to Mike. He has taken it very well."

She nodded understandingly. "I will. And I'll tell Mother and Father that I'm sure you've made the right choice."

Then Mike was seating himself beside James. I saw James give him a quick, inquiring glance. Mike responded with a wry grimace.

"Not my lucky day. Let's go!" Mike said briefly.

James cast a startled look at me, as if he couldn't believe I had rejected a proposal from such a highly eligible bachelor. Then, with a shrug of his shoulders, he let out the clutch.

I stepped back, waving. It gave me a pang to watch the car disappearing down the drive. I had never felt closer to Dorothea than I had since we had come to Port Petroc. I was going to miss her staunch loyalty and affection. I was on my own now. I mustn't, if I could possibly help it, draw Adam into the inevitable battle of wills between me and my grandmother.

I turned reluctantly back into the house. On impulse I ran upstairs to get my mother's only letter to me. It might be that her daughter's words could reach Katherine where mine had failed.

She was still seated on the sofa in the drawing room. She greeted me with an expectant smile, which faded when she saw that I was alone.

"Where's Mike?" she demanded.

"Gone," I answered.

"Gone? Without waiting for our congratulations?" she said like a disappointed child. "I wanted to make plans for the wedding. We must have the reception here, of course."

"I'm sorry, Grandmother, but when I'm married, I'll be married in Kelchester by Father. It will be a quiet wedding with just Dorothea and my best friend, James' sister, and perhaps Kay as bridesmaids. I expect Mummie will give a small reception for us, but we don't want anything in the way of a big show," I said, divining intuitively that Adam would feel as I did about that. "I'm sure Mummie will be glad if you and Aunt Monica will come."

"I wish you wouldn't call Mrs. Haughton 'Mummie.' She's

no blood relative of yours," Katherine said sharply. "You're a Trevinion and the Trevinions are always married from this house."

"I'm also a Haughton, and an Amberton," I reminded her.

She silenced me with an impatient gesture.

"Don't be difficult, child! Mike is willing to let me stage the wedding if his parents agree, and why shouldn't they? It's for the bride's relatives to make the arrangements."

Seamus had gone out again immediately after lunch. I had noticed this weekend, since James and Mike had turned up, that Seamus had been avoiding me. He seemed to have realized that he hadn't a hope of reliving his first and only romance, with me as a substitute for my mother. It was obvious, though, that he resented my indifference to him and the idea of my being wooed by a man half his age. I had caught him several times staring at me with unmistakable hostility. So, I imagined, had Monica. Her manner toward me had thawed considerably. She was eyeing me now with a hint of compassion.

She said wryly, "You might as well save your breath, Lyra. Your grandmother always gets her own way in the end."

"This time, I'm afraid she'll be disappointed," I answered as calmly as I could. "I am engaged to be married—and blissfully happy about it—but I'm not engaged to Mike O'Donnell."

I heard Kay draw a quick breath, as if in relief. Monica raised her brows. Katherine looked at me in undisguised vexation.

"Not to Mike? Why not? Surely you can't prefer a dull dog like James Mallard? Playing for safety? I thought better of your spirit than that."

"On the contrary, I'm sticking my neck right out, Grandmother. Just as my mother did," I told her. "I'm going to marry Adam Denver."

The storm broke then. I had been prepared for her disappointment and anger, but not for the invective which she hurled at me like a rain of hailstones. I had known that Queen

185

Katherine disliked to be thwarted, but I hadn't realized how savage her reaction could be. It was clear to me now why my mother had shrunk from facing her. From one's own mother, such angry, bitter words would have been intolerably painful. It was different for me, as Adam had said earlier. Katherine had no power to wound me. On the contrary, her heightened color, quickened breathing and uncontrolled temper aroused a genuine compassion in me.

"Please—" I said impulsively, when she paused for breath. "Please don't upset yourself like this, Grandmother. It's very bad for you. Anger can be dreadfully exhausting, and you haven't really recovered from the accident yet. You'll make yourself ill."

"And leave you unmoved?" Monica gave a sudden, brittle laugh. "I have to admire your nerve, Lyra, even if I can't admire your choice. What in the world has that young parson to offer you?"

"All I want. A love to match my own. A faith to strengthen mine. A shared life in which we can walk and work together, side by side," I answered steadily. "More than anyone else in this world can offer me."

"You've a strange sense of values," Monica said cynically.

"A grossly distorted sense," Katherine said sharply. "If you persist in this folly, I shall disown you. You can go back to those foster parents of whom you think so much. And you won't be able to touch a penny of the capital your grandfather left in trust for Grace and her children until you're thirty. You didn't foresee that, did you? He didn't intend us to be hurt and disappointed again. He inserted a clause that the capital was to remain tied up until our grandchildren were thirty, unless or until they married with our consent. Your ambitious, fortune-seeking parson should have checked up on the terms of the trust before he proposed to you."

The glint of triumph in her eyes shocked me, and yet deepened my pity for her.

"Oh, Grandmother, won't you try to understand? Money isn't involved. If I ever receive any from the trust, I'll regard it simply as a trust—not as a weapon or a source of pride.

Money can be useful, but wealth is something I've never had or coveted," I said candidly. "Happiness is vastly more important."

"You talk like a fool, child! Do you imagine you'll find any happiness as the wife of a penniless young parson? What prospects are there for Adam Denver if he dares to incite my undying enmity by stealing my granddaughter? Don't underestimate the Trevinion influence!" Katherine warned me.

"You have a certain amount of power, Grandmother, but it can't be compared with ours. The Bible says, 'As having nothing and yet possessing all things.' The things we value are things you can't take away from us," I said quietly. "I'm your granddaughter, but I'm my mother and father's daughter. They would approve of my choice; I haven't any doubt about that."

"So, my disapproval doesn't matter?" Katherine said bitterly. "You can reject my affection and all I was eager to do for you without a qualm? That's the Christian spirit, is it?"

"No, I'm truly sorry that I have to disappoint you. I'm deeply sorry for you because I'm sure there can be no peace or comfort for you while you're driven by your own indomitable will." I saw her lips curl as if she were daring me to pity her. I went on desperately, "I don't know how to say it without sounding smug or critical. It's a question of values. Perhaps you had better read my mother's letter."

"Grace's letter? You have a letter from Grace?"

I nodded. I drew the letter from my cardigan pocket and handed it to her. She took it and hesitated. There was a sudden silence. Then, with an unexpected display of tact, Monica rose and went out through the French windows onto the terrace. Kay glanced at me. Then she, too, sprang up and headed for the door into the hall.

I sat motionless, watching Katherine as, very slowly, she unfolded the letter and began to read it. I saw the hot flush of anger fade from her cheeks. Her firm lips quivered. When at last she raised her eyes to mine, there were teardrops glistening on her lashes. They brimmed over and fell onto the letter.

She said in a strained, shaky voice, "How could she say that she never knew real happiness and peace of mind here with us? Her father and I adored her. We gave her everything any girl could want."

"Everything except the 'unsearchable riches'—the joy and the faith to which my father led her," I said, my heart aching for her, because she looked so hurt and bewildered, as if her daughter's letter had stabbed her to the heart. "If you would try to see it from her point of view, Grandmother, you could be glad for her."

"How can I? It's too late. I'm too old," she said painfully, and again tears welled up in her eyes, slowly, as if over the years she had lost her capacity to weep. "If only she hadn't left us like that—if she had explained—if she had trusted us instead of cutting herself off from us and robbing us of her child—"

Her voice trailed away. I saw her throat muscles contract as if she were swallowing a lump in her throat. I couldn't bear to see her in such distress. It seemed all the more painful because she was obviously struggling hard not to give way to it.

I got up on an impulse which I didn't stop to analyze. I dropped down beside her chair and put my arms around her slight, shaking shoulders.

"Don't, please! Don't grieve about it now. Remember that she was very young and very much in love. I expect she was afraid of hurting you, or afraid that your anger and reproaches would cast a cloud over her happiness and recoil on the man she loved," I said in a rush. "Remember that she hadn't been brought up to face stormy weather. I felt bitter at first, because she had given me to strangers when I might have been with her own family, but I understand now."

For a moment or two, she seemed to brace herself as if she would thrust me away from her. Then, suddenly, she relaxed against me. The thin clawlike fingers of her uninjured hand closed over mine and clung to them.

"Help me!" she gulped, and I could guess what that appeal must have cost her. "Make me understand, Lyra. What did she mean about 'the true riches'?"

* * *

Mary's letter was just like her, full of affection and calm common sense. I smiled as I read it, and then sighed with sudden nostalgia for the old, so much less complicated days at Kelchester. Only, in life one couldn't turn back. One had to go on, and I knew my place was here.

"It's wonderful news about your grandmother's change of heart. I'm sure it was the result of prayer. Remember, 'to Him be the glory,' and don't let her reliance on you turn your head," Mary had written in her frank manner. "It's certainly true that God works in a mysterious way. It wouldn't surprise me if you heard some startling news from Thea quite soon. I always hoped that I might have you or Thea for my sister-in-law, but James seems likely to remain a cautious old bachelor. Thea—hold your breath!—has been seeing a lot of Mike O'Donnell. I gather that he was immensely impressed as well as staggered that you could turn him down for a man in Adam Denver's position. He appealed to Thea for enlightenment, and she has been putting in some real missionary work on him."

I caught my breath at that. My young, gauche, shy sister and the poised, self-assured Mike? It sounded like a fantastically improbable combination.

"Father came home from the office this evening absolutely astounded because Mike had been to see him and announced that he had withdrawn his statement to the police. He's going to let your version stand unchallenged," Mary's letter continued. "He admitted frankly that it was your sister who had induced him to tell the truth and take his medicine. I was right about Thea, wasn't I? Behind her awkward, diffident manner, she's the archdeacon's daughter, and your mother's too. Mike has evidently seen her as she really is, and is genuinely drawn to her. His parents are delighted."

They would be, of course, I thought swiftly. They had been foolishly overindulgent to their only son, but he had obviously been a great anxiety to them. The mayor had a reputation as an honest and public-spirited man. He wouldn't oppose or deride Dorothea's standards. He would be thankful if she could lead Mike into sharing her faith. She would, too, if I knew her. She would, if she loved Mike, use the power he had offered me much more widely than I could have done.

"About your own plans, my dear. I think it is appropriate for you to be married in Adam's church. I'm glad that your father and mother have agreed. Yes, of course, we'll all come down for the wedding and I shall look forward to being a bridesmaid, and to meeting your cousin, Kay."

I refolded Mary's letter and opened Mummie's. I still retained my childish habit of keeping the best to the last. Mummie's, as always, breathed her unfailing love and understanding. It had been she who had persuaded Father that they should give my grandmother her way about our wedding, and that he could marry us in the church at St. Petroc's.

Mummie, too, touched on the growing friendship between Dorothea and Mike. She had been anxious about it at first, she confessed, but said, "Thea is being very sensible. She insists that she must finish her course at the college before there can be any question of an engagement. That will give Mike a chance to settle down to work and to convince her that he's in earnest."

"We were greatly relieved to hear that your cousin, Jay, was making such good progress. If his sister really wants to train as a nurse, we've a suggestion. She could train at the Kelchester Hospital and live with us. I imagine it would be a weight off your grandmother's mind to know that we were looking after her, and she would be company for Thea, who is obviously missing you. What do you think?"

"I think the idea is just like you, Mummie darling," I said aloud. "Kay will jump at it, and Grandmother won't have to worry about her being on her own."

Then I heard a blessedly familiar tap-tap-tap on the French windows. I sprang up eagerly. It was wonderful to know that Adam was welcome in this old house now; that Katherine was turning to him as to another grandson.

Hers had never been a "half and half" nature. Once she had surrendered, she had surrendered herself wholeheartedly. With the same zeal she had shown for the running of the

190

estate, she was now concerning herself with the parish. The bewildered tenants and estate workers, discouraged for so long from attending church, now found themselves sternly rebuked if they stayed away. Katherine was liable to be something of a problem still, but Adam seemed able to cope with her. He had tolerance, patience and a pleasing sense of humor, I had discovered. He could also be quite as determined as my grandmother, but without any heat or loss of temper.

I ran to him, and he put his arms around me, holding me to him. For a moment, our lips clung together. Then I drew him down onto the settee.

"Letters!" I said, waving them at him. "Such lovely letters. Mary and James and their parents will come down for our wedding, and Mary has agreed to be a bridesmaid. And Mummie has a grand idea for Kay—"

With Adam's arm around me, I reread those two letters and he read them with me.

"Isn't it wonderful how everything is working out? If only Seamus would realize how faithfully Aunt Monica has loved him all these years and ask her to marry him, I could be happy about them too," I said impulsively. "As it is, he still seems to think that Grandmother has gone slightly round the bend, and will come to her senses later. He still resents me—and acts as if I've bewitched her."

"Patience, my love! Give him time," Adam answered, with his heartwarming smile. "It isn't easy for a man of his age to revise his whole outlook in a flash."

"Grandmother did. It's like a miracle to have her with us instead of against us. I hope my mother knows. It was her letter which brought me here, and her letter which broke down Grandmother's stubborn resistance," I reminded him. "I was just her messenger."

"And her daughter. Daughter of Grace," he said tenderly— as Mary had said, all those weeks ago in Kelchester. "My love—my dearest love."